SANTA SHORTBREAD

SANTA SHORTBREAD

AUNTIE CLEM'S BAKERY #12

P.D. WORKMAN

Copyright © 2019 by P.D. Workman

All rights reserved.

No part of this book may be reproduced in any form or by any electronic or mechanical means, including information storage and retrieval systems, without written permission from the author, except for the use of brief quotations in a book review.

ISBN: 9781989415689 (IS Hardcover)

ISBN: 9781989415672 (IS Paperback)

ISBN: 9781989415641 (Kindle)

ISBN: 9781989415658 (KDP Paperback)

ISBN: 9781989415665 (ePub)

pdworkman

ALSO BY P.D. WORKMAN

Auntie Clem's Bakery

Gluten-Free Murder

Dairy-Free Death

Allergen-Free Assignation

Witch-Free Halloween (Halloween Short)

Dog-Free Dinner (Christmas Short)

Stirring Up Murder

Brewing Death

Coup de Glace

Sour Cherry Turnover

Apple-achian Treasure

Vegan Baked Alaska

Muffins Masks Murder

Tai Chi and Chai Tea

Santa Shortbread

Cold as Ice Cream

Changing Fortune Cookies (Coming soon)

Hot on the Trail Mix (Coming soon)

Recipes from Auntie Clem's Bakery

Reg Rawlins, Psychic Detective

What the Cat Knew

A Psychic with Catitude

A Catastrophic Theft

Night of Nine Tails

Telepathy of Gardens

Delusions of the Past

Fairy Blade Unmade

Web of Nightmares

A Whisker's Breadth

Skunk Man Swamp (Coming Soon)

Magic Ain't A Game (Coming Soon)

Without Foresight (Coming Soon)

Zachary Goldman Mysteries

She Wore Mourning

His Hands Were Quiet

She Was Dying Anyway

He Was Walking Alone

They Thought He was Safe

He Was Not There

Her Work Was Everything

She Told a Lie

He Never Forgot

She Was At Risk

Kenzie Kirsch Medical Thrillers

Unlawful Harvest

Doctored Death (Coming soon)

Dosed to Death (Coming soon)

AND MORE AT PDWORKMAN.COM

For all of the nurturers

*E*rin spoke to young Peter Foster as he bent close to the bakery display case, examining the newest gluten-free treats with his younger sisters.

"What are you going to make for Christmas?" he asked. "You made lots of really good cookies last year."

"We will again this year," Erin assured him. "I just met with Charley, my partner, on the weekend. We have a nice list of what we are going to have for you this year. We're going to do some of the little one-bite desserts like we had at Thanksgiving."

She saw the disappointment chase across his face.

"I know you didn't like the pumpkin tarts and gingerbread, but that won't be all that we have. And there will be lots of different kinds of cookies. I'm going to make some cutout shortbread cookies. You'll like those, and we can do all kinds of fun shapes."

"Christmas shapes?"

"Yes, of course. Stars and trees and gingerbread men and snowmen. All kinds of things."

"Santa?" one of the little girls asked, bouncing up and down. Her sticky fingers were on the glass of the display case and either Erin or her assistant Vic was going to have to clean it again after they left, but Erin didn't mind. She loved her littlest customers, the Fosters especially.

Erin looked at Vic and glanced at Mrs. Foster to see what they thought. Vic had warned her against using too many secular symbols of Christmas. Bald Eagle Falls was in the Bible belt, and they had to be careful not to offend the customers who didn't want to see pagan symbols or a lot of commercial crap around their religious holiday.

"I'm sure we can do some Santas," Vic agreed and, after a moment Mrs. Foster nodded too. The kids had won that round. They were so inundated through the media that they couldn't be expected to be completely blind to Santa and the other commercial offerings.

"And the Grinch?" Peter demanded. "You have to do the Grinch!"

Erin laughed. "Hmm. I'll have to see what I can find. We're going into the city to look for some new cookie cutters, and I'll have to see if I can find a Grinch. I haven't seen any around."

"That would be cool. We'd buy them."

"The Grinch is green," Karen contributed.

"Yes, I would have to make green cookies or frosting," Erin agreed.

"Green cookies! You can't make green cookies!"

"I certainly can."

"How?"

"Magic," Erin teased. Then, thinking better of the comment, changed her mind. "Just with green food coloring, Karen. It's really easy."

"I haven't had green cookies before."

"Then I'll have to make some for sure, won't I? What did you guys want today?"

They made their choices for the kids' cookie club and Vic handed them out. Mrs. Foster ordered the baked goods she would need for the week and stood with her hand on her slightly-protruding belly while she waited for it all to be wrapped up and totaled.

"I know I've said it before, but I can't thank you enough for all of the lovely gluten-free baking you do. I used to have to do so much extra baking to make something safe for Peter so that he could have something other than the packaged baking from the city. And half the time it didn't even turn out. I always felt bad that he didn't have any choices and just had the same kind of cookies and bread over and over again. Now… it's just so nice to come here and know that he can have anything in the bakery, and it's all so good!"

Erin flashed a look at Peter. "Even if he doesn't like pumpkin pie!"

"Mom says lots of kids don't like pumpkin pie."

"But I do," Mrs. Foster assured Erin. "And I much prefer yours to the ones at the grocery store!"

When the Fosters had gone, there was a lull. Vic went around the display case to wipe down fingerprints.

"I'll be right back," Erin told her. "I need to fix my hair."

Several dark strands had escaped her hairpins and baker's hat, so Erin ducked into the commode to look in the mirror while she took care of it all and then washed up again. Vic, with her long, blond hair, seemed to be able to manage to keep hers tidy and out of her face all day, but Erin frequently had to take a break at some point to get hers back in order. Maybe she should grow hers longer so that she could pull it into a ponytail or bun rather than trying to keep the shorter locks pinned back.

She returned to the front of the bakery, looking presentable again, and smiled at the approaching customers. It was getting noticeably busier as Christmas approached and people were buying more baking for parties, presents, and preparing ahead for their Christmas meals.

Melissa was one of the latest customers. She gave Erin a broad smile and stepped up eagerly to look into the display case. While she lived alone, Erin knew that she would be hosting a dinner for some of the other single women in her church group, and later on Christmas day would be off to the penitentiary to see her friend, Davis Plaint. Melissa never referred to him as a boyfriend or in a romantic way, and wouldn't mention him in front of the other church ladies. Erin often found herself puzzling over their unusual relationship.

"What would you like today?" Erin asked. "Need anything for the department?"

"I think it would be nice if someone other than me sprang for muffins for the police department now and then," Melissa said with an irritated shake of her head that set her dark spiraling curls bouncing. "I only work there part-time, so my paycheck is lower than anyone else's. Maybe Clara or the sheriff could buy them sometime."

Vic's eyebrows climbed. "I always thought you got reimbursed for those."

"No, it's just out of the kindness of my heart. Seems to me it's time for someone else to buy them this time."

Erin nodded uncomfortably. She had taken muffins over to the police department herself occasionally but like Vic, she had always thought that Melissa's purchases were covered by her employer. She would mention it to Officer Terry Piper when she saw him later in the day. She was sure they didn't mean to take advantage of Melissa; probably no one had ever thought twice about it. "Something for you, then?"

"A person can only do so much," Melissa muttered. "With all that I do for the department, they could show some appreciation."

"Yes," Erin agreed. "Everyone likes to be recognized for what they do. Anything interesting going on lately?"

Erin didn't usually encourage Melissa's gossip about the police department or crimes going on in Bald Eagle Falls, but she felt the situation called for a little distraction.

Melissa leaned forward. "Actually…" She looked dramatically left and right to see if anyone were listening in. There were customers behind her, but they were waiting patiently and didn't appear to be eavesdropping. Though Melissa put on a show of being discreet, she preferred an audience. "Have you heard of the Grinch?"

"We were just talking to the Fosters about the Grinch," Erin laughed. "They want me to make green Grinch cookies for Christmas."

"No, not the Dr. Seuss character. The *real* Grinch."

Vic leaned on the display case. "There is no real Grinch."

Melissa nodded vigorously. "There is. At first, we didn't think it was anything more than the usual holiday thefts. You know, there are always a few cars broken into, usually in the city. People leave newly purchased gifts in full view and then are surprised when someone breaks into their car in the parking lot. But Bald Eagle Falls has had an unusual rash of thefts the past couple of weeks."

"What counts as a rash of thefts?" Erin asked.

"I don't know for sure how many have been reported; I haven't filed all of the reports. But there have been house and car thefts, with some pricey items stolen."

"More than normal."

"There are always some. But there have been a couple of families…" Melissa frowned and shook her head. "They've lost all of their Christmas gifts. Folks in this part of Tennessee are not wealthy; some families really have to scrape to get a few things together for the little ones. And when someone like the Grinch comes along and takes everything away… there's nothing they can do. They can't afford to replace them."

"Oh… what about their homeowner's insurance—can't they make a claim?"

"Even if they can, if their deductible isn't too high and it's worthwhile to make a claim, they're not going to get the money in time for Christmas."

"That's so sad!" Vic exclaimed. "Who would do something like that?"

"The Grinch," Melissa said, giving a nod. "You see? Whoever it is, they're stealing Christmas from the children of Bald Eagle Falls."

Erin and Vic shook their heads. Bald Eagle Falls was a small community, close-knit, and it was hard to believe that anyone would want to hurt their neighbors that way. Especially little children.

"That's just terrible." Erin looked down at the products on display. She was mindful of the fact that there were other people lined up behind Melissa, so they couldn't gossip for long. "What do you think you would like today, then? We have chocolate chip muffins." She knew Melissa's weakness for anything with chocolate in it.

Melissa frowned, examining the various possibilities, and then returned to the chocolate chip muffins that Erin had pointed out and decided, "I do think it is a chocolate chip muffin kind of day."

CHAPTER 2

*E*rin knew that Officer Terry Piper was working a modified afternoon shift, and watched to see if he would stop in at Auntie Clem's Bakery while he was on patrol. He and K9 were happy to be getting out of the house after Terry had been sidelined with a head injury and been choked out by an assailant. Neither one of them liked being cooped up all day with nothing to do. But Terry was still suffering from headaches and wasn't yet able to put in a full shift.

Under his old routine, Terry would stop in for water partway through the afternoon on a hot day, and for a cookie and doggie biscuit around closing time. The weather was chilly so close to Christmas, so they didn't need the extra water, but she was still hoping for a visit at the end of the workday, when they would be getting off work as well. But as she turned the sign on the door over to 'Closed,' there was no sign of her boyfriend and his furry sidekick. Vic wiped down the display case.

"No visit from Officer Handsome today?" she teased.

"Doesn't look like it." Erin let out a sigh and left the door unlocked, just in case he came by before they were finished. "Hopefully, that means he went home and not that he's stuck at the office or dealing with a case."

"The sheriff said they'd make sure he didn't work too long."

"Hopefully," Erin repeated.

They fell into the usual rhythm closing out the till, cleaning up, and mixing up batters that would soak overnight for the next morning's muffins and breads.

"Grinch cookies," Vic recalled with a laugh. "I wonder if we'll be able to find some cookie cutters."

"Even if we can't find one that's specifically The Grinch, we could make Santa cookies and give him a green face. It wouldn't be perfect, but people would know what they were supposed to be."

"Perfect," Vic declared. "Great idea."

Erin drove herself and Vic home as usual. Vic lived in the loft apartment over Erin's garage, so when they were on the same shift, they almost always drove together. Vic didn't have a car of her own and was constantly getting after Erin to replace her old clunker. But Erin didn't like to spend more money than she had to, an attitude that had carried over from her lean years, even though she finally had money in the bank from cashing in on a crop of wild ginseng.

"One of these days, it's not going to make it," Vic commented, shaking her head at Erin's car. "It sounds worse than ever."

"I'll take it in for an oil change. That's all it needs."

"It needs a lot more than that," Vic said with authority. "Timing belt. New transmission. The electrical is all screwed up…" She had probably fixed up a lot of cars with her brothers on the farm before she had come out as transgender and been forced to leave home.

"It still runs."

"Until the day it doesn't."

"If I only use it for tooling around Bald Eagle Falls, I'll be safe. If we go out to the city, we can use Terry's or Willie's truck."

"Or you could get a new car."

"Not yet."

Vic shook her head. They walked up the sidewalk together. "Looks like Terry's home. Say 'hi' for me."

"I will. You and Willie going out, or are you going to come over for dinner?"

"We'll do something together. You can have Terry to yourself today."

"Okay. Have a good night, Vicky."

Vic walked around to the back and Erin let herself in the front door. Despite the fact that she had a perfectly good garage, it currently held Clementine's old Volkswagen, so she and the others always parked in front of the house instead.

She gave a mental shrug and walked up to the house. She opened the door and checked the burglar alarm and saw that it had already been disarmed.

"Terry?"

She heard the bathroom door open and Terry walked out of the hall. Orange Blossom darted past him with a yowl. Marshmallow hopped sedately out from behind the couch.

"Hi, guys." Erin bent down to scratch the rabbit's ears and Orange Blossom practically climbed into her arms, complaining loudly. Probably about the presence of K9, who he'd had plenty of time to get used to.

Erin made understanding noises to Orange Blossom, acknowledging his chatter, and looked at Terry with a smile, rolling her eyes.

Terry shook his head. "I think you might be thirty seconds late getting home; he's been pacing around here making a racket."

"Oh, is that the problem?" Erin pressed her cheek against Orange Blossom's head and squeezed him. "Well, I'm here now, so stop complaining."

He instead started with a rumbling purr. Erin scratched his ears. "That's better."

Erin studied Terry's face. "How are you doing?" There were lines around his eyes and he seemed pale. "Are you in pain? Do you want something for your head?"

"Mostly I'm just tired out." Terry thought about it. "Actually, I guess I might need a painkiller too. It's hard for me to tell, sometimes." He pressed his fingers to his temples. "I start feeling tired and foggy, and it takes a while to figure out I've got a headache."

"Let me get one of your pills."

"I can do it."

Erin shook her head. "No, sit down and relax, I'll get you one." She put Orange Blossom down and ignored his renewed complaints as she went into the bedroom and retrieved one of Terry's prescription pills. She got him a glass of water from the kitchen and returned to where he was sitting in the living room. Terry passed his hand over his face, looking slightly gray.

"I don't like to take too many of these," he said, taking it from her and swallowing it down with the water.

"You are allowed to take them when you need them. It doesn't help you to be in pain."

"But it doesn't help me to be dopey either. I don't want to spend the days in a haze."

"If they're too strong, then you can ask the doctor to prescribe a lower dose. But he won't know unless you tell him."

Terry nodded once. "Yes, you're right," he agreed. He went back to rubbing his temples. "I was going to have something ready for us to eat. Or at least to get started on supper."

"Don't worry about it. I can get something ready. You must be hungry."

"Not really. More nauseated than anything."

He had obviously waited too long after his headache had started. Once that nausea had set in, it tended to stay the rest of the evening. He had wanted to lose a few pounds after their cruise but, since the attack, he'd lost more than he should.

"What could you eat? Could I make you a smoothie? Some yogurt? What wouldn't bother your stomach?"

"I don't know. Give it a little while; maybe it will feel better after the pill kicks in."

Erin knew very well that it wouldn't. But he was a grown man and needed to be in control of his own body and life more than he needed her to mother him.

"Okay... but try to have something later. Don't just skip eating."

Terry grimaced, not looking at her. "I'll try. Later."

"And if you want me to go out and get something..." Erin offered. "If there is something you think you could eat..."

"No, you don't need to make a special trip for me."

Erin left him sitting on the couch. K9 was in the kitchen waiting for her, standing close to the cookie jar and looking her way with pleading eyes. He was very well-behaved, but he seemed put out that it had taken her so long to get there.

"Aren't you being patient," Erin crooned. "And such a gentleman. Unlike some animals around here..." She looked pointedly at Orange Blossom, who meowed loudly in exasperation that he hadn't yet received a treat.

Erin got all of the animals treats and checked the fridge for dinner inspiration. Her usual fallback was leftover bread or rolls from Auntie Clem's with some locally-sourced jam. But she was making an effort to take care of her body better and eat something other than straight sugar and carbs, so she made herself look at the vegetables to see if she could put together a salad.

Vegetables were really not her thing, except for the ones that Vic had made at Thanksgiving, with lots of buttery sauces or nuts in caramelized sugar. Those had been really good. But she suspected that the benefits from the vitamins they contained would be counteracted by all of the fat and sugar, which would go straight to her hips and, with her small frame, every extra pound showed.

CHAPTER 3

She returned to the living room with a good-sized bowl of salad and a cold pack for Terry's head. She handed the ice pack to him. Terry looked at it dolefully. He always hated putting it on his head, even though it did seem to provide some relief. He watched her sit down, balancing the bowl on her knees to eat.

"That looks like a particularly virtuous supper."

"Yes, it is," Erin agreed. "If I can fill up on the veggies and not eat bread and jam or ice cream afterward as a reward."

Terry chuckled, the dimple appearing on his handsome cheek. For an instant, the lines on his face smoothed. Then he winced and put the cold pack on the back of his neck.

Erin ate for a few minutes without saying anything, watching him worriedly for some sign that the painkiller and the ice pack were having the desired effect.

"Don't just look at me," Terry complained. "Talk to me. I can still listen."

His eyes were closed, but he could still tell she was looking at him.

"Sorry. Melissa stopped by today."

"Ahh, Melissa. Carrying more news, I assume."

"Did you know she pays for those muffins and everything for the police department out of her own pocket?"

Terry didn't say anything at first. His tone when he spoke again was noticeably different. Not the irritated, slightly sarcastic tone, but more concerned. "No… I didn't know that. I never really thought about it. I always just assumed that it came out of the department's budget."

"It's all her own money. And she's getting kind of annoyed that no one else ever springs for it."

"Well, I guess so. It's not her job to keep us supplied with goodies. Especially not out of her own pocket. She's only a part-timer." He was silent for a minute. "Why doesn't she stop doing it? Sooner or later, someone would either figure out that it was time for someone else to chip in, or that we didn't need them. I don't think anyone ever told her to bring muffins to the department. It was just her own thing."

"Maybe put a bug in Sheriff Wilmot's ear. Have him reimburse her or bring in something himself some time."

"Yeah. I'll try to remember to mention it to him. I'm sure he has no idea that she's getting resentful about it. She may be loose-lipped, but she does her job well and none of us would want her feeling like she wasn't appreciated."

Erin nodded, then remembered he wasn't looking her way. "Yeah. That would be good. I think it would help if she knew it was appreciated and that you weren't all just taking advantage of her kind heart."

"She *is* a kindhearted person."

"Yes." Erin thought about Melissa's relationship with Davis Plaint, currently incarcerated for murder. Was it just that she felt sorry for him? Was there anything else to it? Erin didn't know if she had romantic feelings toward him, or if it was just as Melissa said, a friendship. They had known each other when they had both been in high school and Davis's addiction had kept her from ever having a serious relationship with him then. Did she wish she could rekindle those days? Or was she just being kind to a man she used to know who was down on his luck?

"So, what else did she have to say?" Terry asked. "Or did she just come to gripe about the insensitive jerks that she works for?"

"Oh. She was telling me about your Grinch."

Terry sighed. "Did she tell you that no one knows if the same person is perpetrating these thefts? There is no proof at this point that we have a serial burglar."

"No, she didn't mention that. She sounded like… it was pretty much a foregone conclusion."

"It's not. She's jumping ahead of herself. It has been suggested, but not by any means proven. We may just have a higher rate of theft this year. Bad elements that moved in with the drug problems. Or people who have hit hard times this year. It isn't necessarily just one person."

"Okay. So maybe we don't have a Grinch. Or maybe we have a flock of Grinches."

He chuckled. "A flock? What's the appropriate collective noun for Grinches? A grunt of Grinches?"

"A grouch of Grinches?" Erin suggested.

Terry nodded. "Or maybe some families are just looking for sympathy or handouts. There isn't always proof that they had these gifts in the first place. They could be using theft as an excuse for the fact that they couldn't get anything for their kids this year."

Erin wrinkled her nose and thought about it. She had lived with families who hadn't had very much around Christmas time, but none of them had ever tried anything like that. Approaching agencies to ask for something, maybe when they didn't deserve it or qualify for it, but not flat-out lying and saying that the presents they bought had been stolen.

"I don't know. That sounds a little far-fetched. Did something happen to make you think so?"

"No. It's just another possibility. The claims haven't all been processed yet. If people pay with cash that they've been socking away all year and leave the receipts in the bags with the merchandise, how do they prove what they bought in the first place?"

"But you must be able to tell whether the cars or houses have been broken into, though."

"Not always. A lot of them seem to be opportunistic, taking advantage of an unlocked door. We've had a couple of broken windows, but in other cases, nothing. They're not all the same MO."

"Hmm." Erin nodded. "I guess that's why you don't want to call them serial burglaries."

"There hasn't been anything that appears very violent or personal about any of them. No graffiti or wanton destruction of property. Nothing that would suggest it was addicts or ex-boyfriends."

"And has it all been high-priced items? Things that are worth stealing?"

"In most cases… it has been everything. High-priced and low-value items, everything just swiped at once."

"Like The Grinch."

"No. Not like The Grinch," he said firmly. "We don't have a Grinch. We have a *burglar.* Or burglars. Don't romanticize it."

"Oh, I didn't mean it that way. Yeah, okay. I won't do that. Peter Foster and his sisters want us to make Grinch cookies this year. So it was already on my mind when Melissa came by. I didn't mean to encourage her."

"It's not your fault; someone had already suggested the nickname. But we're trying to keep it under wraps until we decide whether it is one burglar or several people acting independently."

"Okay. I'll make sure I don't repeat it in front of anyone." Erin put the remainder of her salad to the side, unable to finish it. Orange Blossom promptly jumped up into her lap and tried to shove his head into the bowl. Erin pushed the bowl farther away. "You don't want that, silly. Come here and cuddle."

He settled into her lap and started kneading with his paws, his rumbling purr starting up again.

CHAPTER 4

$\mathcal{E}$rin didn't have to say anything to anyone about the possible Grinch; it soon became apparent that the word was spreading quickly through town. Erin wasn't sure whether that meant that more people had been talking about it than just Melissa, or if her gossip had caught fire and was spreading that fast. It seemed like within a day, everyone was talking about the burglaries and the missing presents.

"Who would do such a thing?" Bella asked when she was on for her weekend shift. "Stealing presents from families, from little kids… that's really dirty. How are they going to have Christmas without something for their kids?"

Lottie Sturm, friends with Bella's mother, was close enough to hear Bella and shot her a disapproving look.

"You know that Christmas doesn't have anything to do with gifts. It's about the birth of Jesus. Without him, there is no Christmas."

"I know that," Bella said, a red flush rising from her neck. She was fair-haired and fair-skinned, and the blush was immediately noticeable. "I just meant that… it's what kids look forward to, and for a lot of them, that's the only time they get something really nice. Because it's such a special time of year. So if they don't get anything… it's just sad."

"It is," Erin agreed. She never had been able to understand the connection between the birth of the babe in the manger with Santa Claus and giving wrapped gifts and eating turkey for dinner. "Families that spend all year scraping by to be able to buy something nice for their children shouldn't have to face losing them and not having any way to celebrate the season. No matter what their beliefs are. It isn't fair to the children."

"There are children all over the world who don't have Christmas gifts," Lottie said dismissively. "It is not a part of worshiping Christ."

Erin rolled her eyes and didn't try to explain her position any further. It was hard enough dealing with Bible bashers the rest of the year. They seemed to be all the more zealous as Christmas approached. Erin had never been one to be insulted by anyone wishing her a Merry Christmas, even though she did not believe in any god or religious tenets. But some of the evangelists in Bald Eagle Falls had been getting on her nerves lately. She let everyone else live by their religious beliefs; she didn't see why they had to be so pushy just because she didn't share them.

"It's just not right," Bella agreed.

"It isn't any more wrong to steal Christmas presents than it is to steal the rest of the year or to steal from a corporation instead of a family," Lottie pointed out. "Either way, they are breaking the same laws and commandment. It's the same thing."

"But it seems a lot worse when children are being hurt, don't you think?" Erin asked.

"I don't know if I would say that," Lottie maintained. "It's a sin either way."

"I thought Jesus said it was worse to commit sins against children."

Lottie opened her mouth to argue, then closed it again. "I don't know," she said stiffly.

Erin handed her the bag of bagels she had ordered. "You enjoy those, now. And let me know what you want for Christmas dinner, if you're having anything special. I'm trying to make sure that I have everything prepared that people are going to need. It's not a preorder, you don't have to commit to anything; I'm just trying to ballpark what we are going to need so that we don't end up with too much of one thing and not enough of another."

Lottie nodded briefly and took the bagels. "I'll think about it," she agreed.

When she was out of the store, Bella gave a little giggle. "I think you know more about Christianity and what it says in the Bible than you let on," she told Erin. "You pretend that you don't know anything about what our beliefs are, and then you come out with something like that."

"I wasn't exactly quoting scripture," Erin said, her face getting a little warm. "I don't know exactly what Jesus said about little children. I just remember learning some story in Sunday School… and there are lots of paintings of him with kids. I don't remember the details."

Bella nodded. "Yes, 'suffer the little children to come to me' and talking about not offending them. Better to be thrown in the sea with a millstone around your neck… something like that."

"See, that's pretty drastic," Erin said, nodding.

Bella adjusted the spacing of the baked goods in the display case. "I think that was the point."

"So then the person who is stealing from kids is doing something worse than if they were shoplifting or stealing copper wire."

Bella nodded. "If you believe those scriptures, yes."

Erin nodded, satisfied.

The next morning, Willie walked into the kitchen of Erin's house and looked around at the flour and cookies covering every horizontal surface. He smiled.

"This looks like fun."

Erin wiped her sweaty forehead with the back of her arm. "We're working," she corrected. Then she gave a shrug. "But yeah, it is fun."

"You've got a little smudge…" Willie told Vic, indicating her chin.

Vic put her hands on her hips. "I've got a little smudge?" she repeated. "This from the guy so stained you'd have to remove the first three layers of skin to find any pink?"

Willie's mining and processing work always left him looking grubby, even though he was good about washing. Whatever methods he used in processing his own minerals left his skin stained dark, which probably contributed to the Bald Eagle Falls opinion that he was the equivalent of a homeless bum, when it was actually a testament of his dedication to his work.

Willie looked at his hands as if he'd never noticed this fact, and grinned proudly. "So, which samples are ready for testing?" he asked, looking around at the various batches of cookies.

"We're experimenting with the colors," Erin said, "they'll all taste the same."

"I think somebody had better test them anyway. Just to be sure." He grinned.

"You'd better save room for supper," Vic warned.

"Why, what are you making?" Willie feigned innocence.

"You're in charge of supper tonight and it better be more than just canned soup!"

"What's wrong with canned soup?"

"Nothing, if you're making lunch for your ten-year-old. When you're making dinner for your girlfriend, something more sophisticated is expected."

"Then I'm going to need enough energy," he pointed out. "A man needs calories after a long day's work, if he's going to have enough energy to make a nice dinner."

Vic rolled her eyes at Erin.

"There's a plate over there," Erin motioned to the counter by the fridge. "Those are the freebies. Everything else is necessary for our scientific endeavors."

Willie strode over and grabbed a couple of green cookies before Erin could change her mind. He took a small bite of each and nodded his head. "Definitely edible."

"They'd better be more than edible," Erin told him.

"I'll have to think about it." Willie took another bite as he headed toward the back door. "Dinner at seven?" he suggested to Vic.

Vic wiped at the smudge on her chin. "Yeah, that sounds good."

He exited and walked across the yard to Vic's loft apartment above the garage. Erin shook her head. "Edible!"

"They're delicious," Vic agreed, "but some of them look pretty disgusting."

"Yeah. It's one thing to offer a lime green cookie. It's quite another to make them puke green."

Vic giggled. They continued to work, making careful notes of the amounts of coloring in each small batch of dough to come up with just the right color in the finished cookies.

CHAPTER 5

It was dark when Vic headed home for supper, and Erin puttered around the kitchen tidying away the last few bowls and implements. There was a tap on the back door. Erin looked through the narrow window in the door and let in Adele, the tall, slim redhead who acted as Erin's groundskeeper in the woods behind the house and, in exchange, was allowed to live in the summer cottage on the property.

"Adele, come on in."

Adele still seemed to be avoiding Vic as much as she could. They had all been together for Thanksgiving dinner. Adele had been visibly uncomfortable, but had done her best to be a gracious guest and not show it. Vic, who had been the victim of Adele's estranged husband, was not at all awkward about being with Adele, which seemed to Erin to be a little backward. But Adele was keenly aware of her husband's misdeeds and self-conscious around Vic.

"Evening, Erin." Adele looked around the kitchen. She went to a tray displaying a series of different cookies in varying shades of green and looked down at it. "There seems to be something wrong with your Santas. I think they might be ill. Is it flu season already?"

Erin laughed. "Yes, he's looking rather green around the gills," she agreed. "What do you think of our Grinch?"

"Is that what it is? Yes, I can see that. Once they are decorated. Not bad."

"It was Peter Foster's request. I think all of the kids will like it, anyway. Have you heard about our real-life Grinch?" Erin bit her lip after saying it, remembering that she was not supposed to be spreading gossip about the Grinch around. But Adele was her groundskeeper. She was like a security guard. She was Erin's eyes and ears in the woods and should know about any crimes being committed in the area so that she knew what to look for.

"Your Grinch," Adele repeated blankly, looking around as if Erin might have a new pet she was referring to as the Grinch.

"He's a burglar in the area," Erin explained. "Stealing Christmas presents. So… the Grinch, stealing Christmas, you know."

"Oh. Yes, I might have heard something about that. Have they identified it as one person, then? It's not just the usual holiday thefts?"

"No, the police haven't come out and said that it is a serial burglar. Terry says they haven't been able to figure out whether it is all one person yet."

"So it could just be the usual opportunistic thefts."

"Yes."

Adele nodded. "Well, I haven't seen anything in my neck of the woods. But then, there are not a lot of Christmas presents lying around under those trees."

Erin smiled, nodding and putting away the last few utensils. "I guess not." She turned back toward Adele. "I guess you don't celebrate Christmas, do you?"

Adele kept her affiliation as a practicing Wiccan under wraps, having already been run out of at least one town for being a witch, something that was not well-tolerated in the small Bible-belt towns. She kept to herself and was regarded by the townspeople as being a wise woman knowledgeable in the use of herbs, but kept her actual identity a secret.

"I observe Yule. Winter solstice. It shares a lot of symbology with Christmas, since the Christians chose to borrow the older pagan traditions and repurpose them."

"Do you get together with anyone else to celebrate? It must get kind of lonely living here and not having anyone who shares your beliefs."

Adele studied Erin for a moment, her eyes shrewd. "It can be isolating when you don't have others who share your beliefs… or your lack of beliefs."

"Yeah." Erin let out a stifled sigh. She did sometimes feel rather alone in her own beliefs.

"I maintain a network of friends and practitioners I keep in contact with remotely," Adele explained. "Phone calls, texts, emails. These old-school communications called letters. I am comfortable with keeping my practice personal, for the more part. There are gatherings that I can travel to, if I want to. Maybe sometime I will. But not this year, I don't think."

"That's good. I know you don't want to… *come out,* if that's what you would call it. But maybe you would be able to find more people around here who share your beliefs, if they knew what they were."

"Is that what you have found?"

Erin hadn't exactly found atheists to be popping out of the woodwork to make friends with her because of their shared outlook. Most people in Bald Eagle Falls seemed to either profess Christian values or to keep their mouths shut. Maybe Erin ought to have done the same and not made it known that she was an atheist. But she couldn't imagine trying to live under false pretenses. It would bother her too much to pretend that she was something she was not. Or just to let people think that she was.

"No. I guess not," she admitted.

Adele nodded. "I know Terry is around, so I'm not going to monopolize your time and stay for too long. You've obviously been working hard and you should take some downtime now and spend some time relaxing with him. But I just wanted to mention that I've had… a couple of interesting calls from your sister recently."

"Charley?" Erin tried to think of what Charley would have been calling Adele about. The two didn't exactly run in the same circles.

"Reg Rawlins."

"Oh, Reg."

Reg was one of Erin's former foster sisters. She had made an appearance in Bald Eagle Falls which wouldn't be forgotten any time soon. Her act as a medium who was able to speak with the dead was one thing. Erin didn't approve of the scam. But the disappearing act that she had pulled along with the heirloom jewelry of several clients was quite another thing. The woman had no shame.

"What exactly did Reg want to talk to you about?"

Adele shook her head slowly. "It's a little difficult to follow, sometimes. She seems to have gotten involved with some of the paranormal community out there… I don't know if she's playing them, or they're playing her. Or maybe she's…" Adele looked upward, trying to put her thoughts into words tactfully. "Maybe she's a little bit… different…?"

"Reg has always been different," Erin sighed.

That was an understatement. Reg had driven their foster mother, her social worker, and a myriad of medical professionals crazy trying to figure out how to deal with her. Sometimes she seemed like any other long-term foster child, resigned to the uncertainty of life, doing her best to put on a show of being a good, responsible kid. Testing the limits and chasing new schemes to make money and figure out how she was going to survive once they aged out of foster care. And dragging Erin into her schemes.

And on the flip side, Reg could do magic tricks that freaked Erin out, talked to the air, and acted out so bizarrely that Erin was sometimes sure she was out of her mind.

Adele cocked her head, waiting for further information. Erin sighed. Like Adele, she was trying to be sensitive and politically correct about Reg's more unusual behaviors.

"She has had issues in the past. It's hard to know how to take her sometimes, whether she is putting on a show for you or is… having an episode." Erin shrugged. "I've only heard from her once or twice since she was here, and both times, she sounded kind of… excited."

"Right," Adele agreed. "Quite excited." She put her palms up in a gesture of surrender. "Anyway… she has some kittens that she is trying to find homes for, and she wondered if I wanted one of them."

"Isn't she in—" Erin broke off, remembering that she didn't want to give away where Reg had run to. "She isn't even in Tennessee. If she's trying to give away kittens, she should do it locally. What's she going to do, ship one here?"

"She says they're very special kittens. She's trying to match their personalities up with the people she thinks they would get along with best, and she and the owner of the mother cat are willing to ship one of them here if I want it and they think I would be a good match."

"Don't do it," Erin said immediately. "I don't know what kind of a scam she has cooked up, but don't step into her trap. It will not turn out well."

Adele considered this for a minute, then nodded. "I'll take your word for it. It… didn't feel right, but I thought if she needs help with these kittens and I was thinking about getting a cat anyway…"

"Don't let her talk you into it. You can get a kitten from any of a dozen farms around here, or a stray like Orange Blossom or one that Doc is trying to find a home for. Whatever Reg is up to, it's bound to be some new moneymaking scheme of hers. Maybe she's insuring them and then they get lost in transit, or she's transporting something illegal in the cat carriers. I don't know. She's got something up her sleeve. Believe me, she is not doing this just for the good of the kittens or their owner."

Adele nodded. "Good to know. Thanks for that. I won't get involved, then."

"Do you want to stay for a cup of tea?" Erin offered as Adele started to turn back toward the door.

"Oh, no. You go ahead and take some time with Officer Piper. I am going to walk my rounds."

Erin smiled. It was good to know that someone was keeping an eye on things in her woods, making sure that there weren't teenagers lighting fires or leaving beer cans and other litter behind. She didn't like Adele wandering around alone at night, but that was what Adele wanted, and she was a grown woman capable of making her own choices. Erin felt safer knowing that she was on the job, just like she did with Terry doing his police rounds.

"Okay, have a good night, Adele."

CHAPTER 6

*E*rin tossed and turned restlessly. She tried just to stay still and let sleep overcome her, but Terry had been in and out of bed several times, and it was hard to turn off her worry for him and whether he was still up, pacing restlessly and trying to get his own demons under control, or whether he had fallen asleep in front of the TV and she was the only one still awake and restless.

When she finally drifted off to sleep, her dreams were soon overtaken by visions of Mr. Inglethorpe, one of the most disturbing murder cases she had been exposed to. She relived the horror and disbelief that she had felt when she had seen his body, combined with the terror and despair that had flooded her brain and body when she had realized that Terry had been kidnapped by a crazy woman and could already be dead in a shallow grave or lying injured with his lifeblood draining slowly away. She woke up suddenly, a scream strangled in her throat. She saw a dark shape hovering over her.

She tried to hit, to cry out, to call for help. It wasn't the first time her bedroom had been invaded, and she knew she had to fight for her life if she were going to escape.

"Erin, Erin! It's me. It's okay. You were having a dream. It's Terry."

Erin stopped fighting him off and Terry sat beside her and enfolded her in his arms, holding her close and waiting for her to recover.

Erin broke into sobs, her voice finally released, able to express all of the fear and horror that overwhelmed her. She put her arms around Terry, sobbing into his chest, melting into him.

"It's okay," Terry soothed. "Why don't you tell me about it? Get it out into the open."

She knew that she should; it was the only way to integrate the nightmares with her logical daytime thoughts. The therapists she had seen in the past talked about exposing her fears to the light of day, desensitizing herself so that she could handle the feelings and work through them.

But that operated on the assumption that she could talk about it, that talking about it wasn't just as painful as the nightmares themselves. Talking about it meant not allowing herself to heal from trauma, but continually ripping off the scab that had started to form and making it bleed all over again.

"I'm sorry." Erin tried to wipe her eyes and to stop herself from sobbing. "I didn't mean to wake you up. You had probably just gotten to sleep."

"Don't worry about that." He rocked back and forth slightly and rubbed her back, trying to soothe her. "That's not an issue at all. I'm not working full days. I can have a nap if I need to. I just want you to be okay."

"I'm… I'm okay," Erin sobbed and sniffled.

"Tell me about it." He stroked her hair back from her face.

"Nothing new. Just the same things… the bakery. All of the…" She couldn't bring herself to describe it in detail. She clutched herself to him. "I was so worried when we didn't know where you were." He had heard this often enough to know she had jumped from one story to another. No longer talking about discovering Mr. Inglethorpe, but realizing that Terry was in danger and trying to do something to help him.

"I know you were. I was scared too. It's okay to be scared."

"But not now. Not over and over again. It's over and done."

"It was so big that you weren't able to process it all at once. You're still trying to get through it. To allow yourself to feel it all."

"Is that what you're doing?"

Terry rested his chin on the top of Erin's head and breathed into her hair. "No, I'm trying as hard as I can to avoid feeling it," he said honestly.

Erin giggled. "You're trying to process it too."

"My brain is trying to process it. I don't want anything to do with it. I want to block it all out and not have to feel it anymore."

"Yeah," Erin agreed. She was glad that he could joke about it and be honest with her about what he was feeling. It made her feel just a little bit better about the struggle she was still having.

She wasn't the one who had been hurt. She hadn't been attacked like Mr. Inglethorpe. She hadn't been attacked like Terry and Jack Ward. She had only seen and been a part of the rescue effort. Even then, there hadn't been much she could do but sit and hold Terry's hand or to keep Jack Ward still while they waited for the real professionals to arrive.

Her sobs started to slow and her heart began to beat more normally. The tense muscles of her stomach started to relax, leaving her feeling just a little bit empty and nauseated at the same time. Terry kissed her head, and then pressed her down gently, back into the warm spot in the blankets where she had been sleeping. He continued to rub her back after she was lying down.

"We'll get through it, Erin," he promised. "I don't know how long it's going to take, but we're going to get through it. I don't care if you have to tell me the same dreams a hundred times. Just keep telling me, just keep getting through it. Someday…"

Someday, she'd be able to talk about it and to describe it without the sick feeling in her stomach and the feelings of panic and despair. Eventually, it would just be a story, something she had witnessed, and not a memory that ripped the breath right out of her.

"Will you cuddle with me?"

He moved to the other side of the bed and she knew he was preparing to lie down with her. She always felt better when he was in bed beside her. Except when she knew she was keeping him up with her restlessness. Or when he was swearing under his breath as he tried to find a comfortable position and convince his body that sleep was possible. The doctor had prescribed both of them sleeping pills, but Erin never took hers because she knew they would leave her feeling dopey in the morning, and Terry didn't take his because of some macho feeling that he should be strong enough to force himself to sleep. And he worried that he might be needed at night at some point, even though he wasn't yet back on call.

He cuddled up behind her, molding his body against hers, enfolding her in his arms and breathing in her ear.

"It will be okay. You're going to have a good sleep for the rest of the night. You're not going to have any more nightmares. You will be able to wake up in the morning relaxed and refreshed for the day ahead."

She hoped that the affirmations would have the desired effect on her brain, giving it his 'marching orders' for the night. But she was afraid his words would have no effect at all.

Erin was starting to relax and let her thoughts drift again when Terry's body suddenly jolted. She thought at first that he'd had a 'sleep start,' one of those jerks that she sometimes had as she was starting to fall asleep and then had the sensation of falling and startled back awake. But he turned over and she heard him pick up his phone from the nightstand.

"What is it?"

Terry swore as he read the message that had been sent to him. "There's been another burglary."

"You're not on call."

"No… but they're having everyone available go out."

"Tell them you're not available." She reached out like she could physically hold him back. Like if she just touched him, he would agree to stay with her and not go to the burglary scene. But she knew that he had already made up his mind. He missed the late-night calls, the way that the police department needed him and the citizens of Bald Eagle Falls relied on him. Maybe it was what he needed to do to get his confidence back. Maybe going out to a crime scene was better than staying at home trying to go to sleep when his brain wouldn't quiet down. Maybe it was just the adrenaline rush pushing him into action. A lot of first responders were addicted to that rush. So much that they would make their own excitement if there weren't an actual emergency.

"I can go, Erin. I'm fine. You go back to sleep. You don't need to stay up or worry about me. You have the bed to yourself; I won't be keeping you awake with how restless I am."

He was looking for excuses. Erin slept better when he was there with her.

Most of the time.

Some of the time.

Sometimes she needed him there and nothing else would help her to get to sleep.

"Don't stay for hours. Just long enough to sort things out. Someone else can worry about all of the paperwork and follow up."

"I'll be back as soon as I can," Terry promised. His weight lifted from the mattress and she could hear him pulling on his pants and his duty belt. "But I don't know when that will be. You might be up already before I get back. Just get some sleep and don't worry about me."

He walked around the bed while he slipped his arms into the sleeves of his shirt and started to button it up. He leaned over and kissed her on the cheek.

"It will be okay. I'm not going into anything dangerous. You know that the crime has already been committed and I'm just helping process the scene and get the case moving forward. Nothing is going to happen to me."

"Okay." She didn't argue with him. Her mind immediately went into overdrive, running through the scenarios of all of the things that could happen to him. All of the different ways that things could go terribly wrong on his way to the scene, while he was there, when he was at the police department offices in the Town Center, or on his way home afterward.

Or maybe they would ask him to put in a shift while they investigated the burglary.

She never knew what things might happen while he was away from her. He had a dangerous job and had nearly lost his life the last time. Who knew how many more times he had been in danger that he had not told her about? Who knew how many more he would face before his number was up?

"I'll see you later," Terry promised. "Sweet dreams."

CHAPTER 7

The day dawned, but Erin was already up by that time, at the bakery, working away on their Christmas offerings. There was plenty to be done as the season approached. The children were getting more and more eager and, throughout the town, there was a rising tide of excitement that surprised Erin.

It had never occurred to her that adults—some adults—anticipated Christmas just as much as the little children. She'd never been big on Christmas herself, and when she had aged out and was no longer forced to attend church masses, bickering family dinners, or respite care while the family and their 'real' children went on a nice vacation, she had ceased to mark the day as anything more than a day off of work. When she had been doing home care for seniors, she had often taken extra holiday shifts to cover for someone else who wanted Christmas off to celebrate with their own family.

But in Bald Eagle Falls, the adults often seemed just as eager to buy their children special gifts, arrange big celebratory meals, or plan other holidays to enjoy the time together as a family. It was kind of nice, making Erin think of old movies with snow and sleighs with bells and Christmas trees that reached to the ceiling. People just didn't do Christmas like that anymore. Or maybe in

Bald Eagle Falls they still did, a little pocket of tradition amid commercially catered parties and spoiled brats trying to one-up each other on the best high-tech Christmas haul.

Terry texted Erin just before noon to inform her he was going home and would see her at the end of the day. Erin was glad that he hadn't let the sheriff talk him into working a full day to stay on top of the latest burglary. Or maybe it wouldn't have been Sheriff Wilmot, but Terry talking himself into putting in a full day when his injured brain still wasn't able to do that much work yet. And then he would have a setback and be angry that he couldn't put in the time that he wanted to, and the bitter and disappointed feelings would build until he was impossible to be around.

By the time she headed home, she knew a lot of the details of the latest burglary. It just wasn't possible to keep news from spreading around a little community like Bald Eagle Falls. She hurried home to discuss it with Terry. He might not want to give any details to her, but if she knew them already, he couldn't be blamed for that.

"Can you believe that he had the nerve to steal the Christmas gifts for needy families?" Erin demanded, almost before she was even in the front door. "What kind of a person not only steals families' Christmases, but also steals presents for children who don't have anything else? Who does that?"

Terry was on the couch in front of the TV. He startled at her entrance and rubbed his eyes, blinking at her owlishly. Marshmallow jumped down from his lap and Orange Blossom hurried into the room to get in on the conversation, giving his own input in a loud voice at regular intervals.

"What was that?" Terry asked groggily.

"The children's gifts. Why would anyone do that?"

"I don't think our burglar particularly cares about whose gifts he is stealing," Terry said. He rubbed his eyes. "It seems to be nothing more than where he can get the best haul. And what's better than a charity collection like that? Just load it all into a truck, and head into the city to pawn it or to hawk it on a street corner. Besides, it doesn't exactly belong to anyone. Not yet."

"And you think now that we are dealing with a serial burglar?" Erin asked, noticing that there had been a change in his language.

Terry hesitated. He wasn't revealing the inner workings of the police investigation. He hadn't told Erin anything about suspects or how the burglaries had been committed. He was just answering a general question, one that parents all over Bald Eagle Falls would also want to know the answer to.

"I think," he said slowly, "that we can probably conclude that at this point. This isn't just the normal level of crime seen around this time of year in Bald Eagle Falls from year to year. There is something more sinister at work. Someone who thinks they can get away with this. It's not just opportunistic... it is planned. Carefully orchestrated."

"Who would do something like that?"

"We're going to have to develop a list of suspects. Who knew about the gifts and how to get access to them for each of the burglaries. Any enemies of the families. Who knew their plans at the times the burglaries occurred."

"Because they were all done while the house was empty."

Terry nodded. "Either someone was watching for the houses to be empty, or they knew when the families were going to be away. It's not as easy as you might think to surveil a house for any length of time without people getting suspicious about your activities. People watch out for the neighbors. They don't like strangers sitting in cars for no reason or walking up and down the block somewhere they don't belong."

"So you think it was someone who knew all of the families."

"Or a service provider that was in their homes or had access to their schedules. A cleaner, a dog walker, a carer. People used to pose as telephone repairmen, but cell phones are so ubiquitous now that you don't often see anyone who has anything to do with physical lines. Except maybe in a business. But someone knew when these victims were going to be out."

"And how to get into the Center where the needy children's gifts were being held. They were at the Community Center?"

"Yes. And they're pretty good about not giving out keys without proper documentation. Everyone signs in and signs out. Keys are provided face-to-face, not left in a mailbox. And they have to be returned immediately upon the end of an event. And there is an electronic keypad alarm which they change the code to regularly. It wasn't tripped."

"Was it set?"

"The woman in charge of hall rental swears that it was. But it wasn't set when the police were called. Either it wasn't set, or it was disarmed."

"Or maybe someone cut one of the sensor wires?" Erin suggested, remembering the problems they'd had when her system had been installed.

"We made a thorough check of all of the wiring and sensors. Everything was intact."

Erin rubbed the back of her neck, right below her skull, and thought about that.

*E*rin headed for the front door of the bakery carrying a tray of goodies. She gave Vic a little wave.

"Back in a few minutes, just taking some treats over to Naomi for the book club."

"No problem."

The Book Nook was just a little way down Main Street from Auntie Clem's new location. Erin stepped out into the cool, crisp air of the Tennessee winter, savoring the chance to get away from the warmth of the bakery ovens. The winters in Tennessee—or the one she had experienced so far—had not been nearly as bad as the biting cold of the Maine winters.

The Book Nook had been decorated with garlands and lights, a toy train running in the front window display with various children's books arranged to tempt parents and grandparents to buy books for the kids instead of just the latest electronic gadgets. It was pretty and festive. Vic had put up decorations at Auntie Clem's as well, and while Erin liked them, she did find them a little distracting and would be glad when it was time to put them away again. She preferred the uncluttered lines of the shop to the busy-ness of Christmas.

"Hi, Erin! Merry Christmas!" Naomi greeted in a pleasant

voice, clearly enjoying the season, and maybe the extra money that came in from Christmas shoppers. She didn't sound stressed out by the season, anyway.

"Merry Christmas," Erin returned. "I come bearing sweets."

Naomi approached and looked over the tray of Christmas goodies as she took them from Erin.

"These look just great! Oh, and look at your Grinches! Those are wonderful! Perfect for our discussion today." Naomi motioned toward the chairs that had been set up for the book club.

Erin saw the famous Dr. Seuss book set up together with some other classic Christmas books for children. "That's great! Everyone will think we coordinated it. Very professional of us."

"Hopefully, we'll still get a good group today. Things always slow down a little this time of year with people out shopping, going to kids' recitals, parties, all of the other rush and chaos of the season. How about you—are you all ready for Christmas?"

"Uh..." Erin's face heated. She looked away from Naomi, focusing on the titles of the books in the Christmas display. "I actually don't do much for Christmas. I'll be helping Vic to get Christmas dinner together for us, but... I don't do anything special other than that."

"Oh. That must be a bit of a letdown. You don't do anything?"

Erin shrugged. "I'll take the day off. Auntie Clem's will be closed. But other than that... just the dinner with Vic and the others."

"You don't give gifts? What about Officer Piper? Or Vic? Not even to your closest friends?"

Erin bit the inside of her lip. The year before, they had focused on the dinner and other things that Vic wanted to do. Watching some of the cheesy old Christmas movies on TV. Decorating the bakery and the house. The cookies and treats they had made, which ended up populating her freezer at work and at home for several months. Willie had arranged for Jeremy to visit from Moose River, the first person that Vic had seen from her family since leaving home, and Vic had been over the moon.

There had been the trouble with the dognapping ring and returning animals to their families, which had ended up taking most of the day and had distracted people from the fact that they weren't exchanging gifts. But now that Vic and Willie and Erin and Terry were established couples, would it be different? Would they be expecting Erin to conform and spend her time trying to find the perfect gift for each person in her life?

And if she gave a gift to Vic, would she need to give one to Charley, her sister and business partner? And what about her employees? It had mostly been just her and Vic the previous year and Erin hadn't considered giving Christmas bonuses or a white elephant exchange or special gifts to her other employees. She hadn't planned a Christmas party or even just end-of-year celebration for the bakery workers. They were so busy with making sure they had all of the special Christmas treats customers would be looking for to mark the season; it seemed crazy to be trying to plan a Christmas party too.

"Sorry!" Naomi said. "I didn't mean to upset you. I didn't realize that you didn't do anything for Christmas. I don't know why, but I thought…" she trailed off and gave a helpless shrug. "A lot of people who aren't religious still give gifts and participate in the other traditions of the season. We're always complaining that it's too commercial, too secular. So I hadn't really thought about… what people like you do."

"I never really wanted to get into all of that," Erin explained. "Growing up, Christmases were just so awkward, and I never believed in the 'reason for the season,' so… then I was on my own, and it was just a day off. Or a day I put in extra shifts so that others could get it off."

"Well, you're certainly not required to observe it," Naomi said, putting the tray down and straightening it as if getting the edge perfectly parallel with the counter was vitally important. "I imagine you get enough flak about it from the more… devout ladies."

That was one way of putting it. Maybe Erin had set herself up by agreeing to restart the ladies' tea after church services each Sunday, a tradition that Clementine had started when she was running her tea shop. Erin had thought that it would help the ladies who attended First Baptist to accept her in spite of her atheism. And it had; but it also opened her up to a certain amount of evangelism as they tried to 'encourage' her and Vic to attend church services.

Vic was Christian, but had a pretty good idea of how she would be treated as a transgender woman if she were to attend church in Bald Eagle Falls. She and Willie sometimes went into the city over the weekend and, while Erin had never asked, she suspected that Vic occasionally snuck into a church service where her background was not known.

"I should be getting back to the bakery," she observed, preparing to leave.

"Oh, wait for a minute. Don't run away," Naomi protested. "I wanted to ask for your help with something."

Erin hesitated, hovering between staying to see what Naomi needed and returning to her shop rather than facing the awkwardness of the situation.

"I've been talking to some of the other ladies about doing something for the children," Naomi said.

Erin stopped. "What children?"

Naomi took a step closer to establish a more intimate conversation. "There are several families who have been affected by… the thefts this Christmas. Families that aren't going to be able to recover themselves and give their kids a happy Christmas. And maybe it wouldn't be your thing, seeing as you don't observe Christmas…" Naomi hesitated.

"What are you thinking of doing?" Erin prompted.

Naomi's shoulders dipped in relief. "Well, we're looking at doing some fundraising. Or maybe a toy drive. I'm going to donate some books. Some of these families are really hurting. The kids will just be devastated if they don't get anything for Christmas. How do you tell your children someone stole Christmas and you can't get them anything? We may not be able to replace the electronics that got stolen, but we can give them some of the traditional toys—cars, puzzles, board games, books…"

"Those are probably better for their brain development anyway."

"Yes," Naomi agreed. "So… you're not offended by me asking? Whether you're interested in being involved?"

"Of course not. I remember what it's like to be a kid at Christmas when everyone else is getting special presents, and I was sort of… forgotten or a second thought."

"Oh?" Naomi frowned. "I'm so sorry to hear that."

Erin shrugged. "Obviously, I survived it. It doesn't bother me. Mostly the families I lived with did the best they could. Not every child has an ideal upbringing. But if I can do something to help out some of these little guys to at least feel like someone cares this Christmas, I'll do what I can."

"Thank you so much. We're going to have a meeting over at the school tomorrow night if you can make it. Not until seven, so you have time to close and get a bite to eat. And there will be cookies and refreshments at the meeting." She laughed. "I was going to pick up a bag of store-bought, but maybe I could impose on the baker to bring some day-olds?"

"You can have whatever is left in the case at the end of the day. I always have leftovers."

"Awesome." Naomi's voice squeaked. "I'll see you there!"

CHAPTER 9

They met the next day in one of the classrooms at the school.

Erin hadn't been inside the school before and looked around in interest. It was strangely familiar; a high school room filled with desks and tables much like the ones she had attended, but modernized with technologies that had been developed since she went to school, posters about putting phones away to study, anti-bullying messages, and health messages that were more explicit than anything she had been exposed to at school.

Since it was a high school classroom, the desks were big enough, and though the grown-ups might be uncomfortable sitting in desks once more, they were at least physically accommo-dated. Most of the adults there had grown up in Bald Eagle Falls and had probably attended classes in that very room.

Erin's platters of cookies and other baking were set up at a station with coffee, hot water for tea, and what was supposed to be cold water for drinking but had been left to sit out for too long. Erin circulated, not hungry and not wanting to be corralled in one of the desks until she had to be, and she visited with the other adults, business owners, the church ladies, and some parents from the PTA, who had come to the meeting.

"If we could all sit down," a middle-aged man with graying hair instructed. "The sooner we can get started here, the sooner we can get done and let you folks get back home."

It was a few minutes while everyone broke off from their conversations and found seats. Then the whispering and scraping of chairs ceased and everyone was still.

"For those who don't know me, I'm Vice Principal Fitzroy. I have been asked to coordinate the efforts from the school's point of view. We can help in identifying which families have the greatest needs and share some information on the children—ages, gender, what some of their interests may be—so that we can get them gifts that are targeted instead of just generic toys thrown in a bin."

Erin nodded, having been on the receiving end of generic charity gifts as a child. Cheap stuff usually, a baby doll or some toy that was intended for a much younger child. Nothing that she was genuinely interested in.

"Naomi from the Book Nook has generously offered to donate some books, and we would like to raise some money to pay for some more, and to get some toys, games, clothes, or other gifts as well. We are looking for ideas for some quick fundraising activities since we don't have much time before Christmas and need to start buying the gifts within a few days. Luckily, it's not Christmas Eve, but we're still going to have to be quick and efficient."

"A bake sale?" one of the women suggested.

"A bake sale," Fitzroy echoed, and he turned around to write it messily on the whiteboard. "Do we have volunteers who could contribute something to a bake sale? We want to catch people before they have done all of their shopping for Christmas treats or we're not going to sell much."

A couple of people turned and looked toward Erin, and she nodded. "We can do a few extra batches of cookies to contribute to a bake sale," she agreed.

"Great. And is there any chance you could be in charge of

coordinating others? Gathering everything to a central location, arranging for when and where the sale is supposed to be?"

Erin winced inwardly at being put on the spot. She might not have Christmas shopping to do, but she was already pretty busy with the bakery.

"Uh, let me think about it."

He nodded and wrote her name beside 'bake sale' on the whiteboard. They went on to the next suggestion without further discussion, as if that were all settled. Erin frowned and fished a notepad out of her purse. As they talked about other ideas, she started a list of things that she would need to do if she were in charge of the bake sale.

If she were going to refuse the assignment, then she would need to do it by the end of the meeting so that they could pick someone else. She didn't hear much else that was said as she worked through the logistics of running a bake sale but, in the end, it wasn't too bad a job, and Erin figured she could probably fit it into her schedule with a little help from Charley and the employees at Auntie Clem's.

Eventually, she looked up from her list and at the whiteboard to see the column of other fundraising ideas and names that had been suggested. If they all went ahead, the town would be pouring a lot of resources into those families that had had their gifts stolen or who would have been the targeted recipients of the toys in the needy children's donation bin. But they wouldn't all be able to get off the ground in such a short period of time. Some of the ideas didn't have any names next to them, which meant no one had been volunteered to spearhead them.

She was getting tired as the meeting drew on. Looking at her phone, Erin decided she would give it another fifteen minutes. If things weren't winding down, she was going to have to sneak out anyway. She needed to be up early for the bakery. Other people might not be going to bed until midnight, but she needed to have a few hours of sleep under her belt by that point.

Others were moving around restlessly, feet starting to tap

and desks to scrape the floor as people got tired of sitting. Fitzroy nodded and clapped his hands once. "Okay, please contact the people whose names are on the board to coordinate efforts. We won't be able to get all of these things done, but it should be obvious pretty quickly which ones have the most interest and the best potential. I will be the contact point for the school, for both internal and external communications." He looked around at the room. Everyone nodded. Fitzroy smiled. "Class dismissed."

As everyone got up, the room filling with chatter and movement, he turned around and wiped the ideas off of the board that didn't have any names beside them. Erin quickly jotted down the other fundraisers that might be going ahead and stuffed her notepad back into her bag.

"You're the baker," a big man next to her commented. Erin turned and looked at him. She had seen him around Bald Eagle Falls before, but she didn't know who he was.

"Yes," she agreed, giving a nod of confirmation. "Erin Price. Auntie Clem's Bakery."

"I'll have my wife give you a call. She makes a mean banana loaf. Always sells out at the Founder's Day sale."

"Great, thank you, Mr...?"

"Coach Hadrian."

"Oh, you're the coach of one of the teams here?"

"The coach of *all* of the boys' teams," Coach Hadrian corrected. "That's right. It's a big job, even in a town this small."

"It must be. So you know the families of some of the kids who have been the victims of these thefts?"

Hadrian looked grave. He nodded solemnly. "I've been teaching here for a few years, so I know just about all of the families who have teenagers. I think I know most of those who have been targeted. Sad business."

"It is. I don't think that whoever is behind it understands what it is like for a kid who doesn't have anything... how you handle Christmas when all of your friends are getting presents, some of them really expensive, but you aren't getting anything. Or you're getting new socks and underwear. It's tough on kids."

"That sounds like the voice of experience."

Erin shrugged it off. "I met a lot of other families and kids in foster care. You see how it is."

"I can sympathize with those kids."

"You must, or you wouldn't be here today, right?" Erin agreed. "If you didn't care, you wouldn't bother to show up for this meeting."

"That's right. I feel like these kids are my own, I'd do anything for them. And if I have to eat a few extra cookies and banana loafs, well then…" He patted his stomach, which lapped his belt by a couple of inches, and grinned.

"You'll take one for the cause." Erin laughed.

"Exactly."

Vice Principal Fitzroy approached them. He smiled and slapped the coach on the shoulder and nodded to Erin. "Thank you for your help on the bake sale, Miss Price. It's good to have someone with baking experience and good business sense to take control of that."

Erin's face warmed. She usually thought of herself as a blue-collar worker, someone without any education who provided what services she could with elbow grease and not much else. She wasn't used to being complimented for her business acumen.

"I don't know how much business sense I can claim," she said with a nervous laugh. "It's just what I've learned in running Auntie Clem's Bakery."

"That's exactly what I mean. You run a successful niche business that anyone would have told you would fail here in Bald Eagle Falls. You've got feet-on-the-ground experience, not just book learning or some fancy university; you've done whatever it took to make it work, and you've been successful."

Erin started to sweat, embarrassed at the compliments. She nodded again. "Well… thank you. I appreciate that."

"And we appreciate your help on the bake sale. Your contribution will be invaluable. I see you've met the coach."

"Yes, he was just telling me about his wife's banana loaf."

"Excellent. I hope Shirley will send a few our direction."

"Of course she will," Hadrian assured him.

"It's so sad about the families that have had their presents stolen," Erin repeated to the vice principal. "I'm glad that you're doing something to help the families out. Though it will be hard for a lot of families to donate to the drive, won't it?"

Fitzroy nodded. "This is not a wealthy area, so there are many who are already stretched to the limit. But people are remarkably generous, and will still give their widow's mite."

Erin stared at him, trying to translate his words into something that made sense. "What?"

"The widow's mite."

Erin glanced over at Hadrian to see if he understood the reference, and he apparently did. "It's a story from the Bible."

"Oh. You'll have to tell me about it; I don't know that one."

"Jesus watched people donating money at the temple, and many people were giving huge sums of money and showing off how generous they were with their offerings and, consequently, how rich they were. The widow, though, gave one tiny coin, worth very little. But it was all she had."

Erin nodded. "So she gave the most, percentage-wise."

"Exactly," Fitzroy agreed. "And our indigent families are likely to give more than the wealthier individuals. They know what it's like not to be able to give their kids what they want to, and they will give whatever they can, and more."

CHAPTER 10

$\mathcal{E}$rin broke away from the classroom as quickly as she felt was polite. A lot of parents and townspeople were still talking and visiting, but she didn't know a lot of them and wanted to get home to bed in good time.

It was dark outside the school, but there were lights on in the parking lot and kids playing basketball nearby, so she didn't feel like she was alone or in any danger. The boys' voices and the echoing bounce of the ball seemed familiar and soothing. The air was cold. Not as cold as Maine, but winter had definitely hit Bald Eagle Falls. There was no snow, and likely wouldn't be, which made Erin a little homesick—just a very tiny bit—for the north. There would be a white Christmas in Maine.

"Hey, Miss Erin!" one of the kids called out.

Erin smiled and turned to see who it was. "Oh, hi Harold." Erin nodded a greeting.

Harold Melville was the son of a family that had recently moved to Bald Eagle Falls, all the way from Nashville. Erin hadn't heard their reasons for moving, but didn't think it had been for Mr. Melville's work. He seemed to be still looking for something steady, taking some early shifts at the grocery store and doing some yard work for local families. Maybe they had wanted to get away from bad influences in Nashville, getting their boys away from the drug culture and other temptations until they were older.

Harold was tall and skinny, a celiac like Peter Foster, who had to avoid gluten to stay healthy. He didn't often shop with his mother and, unlike the Foster children, did not participate in the kids' club for free cookies, but he did stop at the bakery after school some days to grab a muffin or granola bar to hold him over until after a game or practice.

"This is Miss Erin," Harold told the other boys. "She's the baker. She makes awesome food."

"At that bakery that burned down?" one of the others asked.

"Yes. We have a new location now, but the old one did have a fire."

The boy nodded. "My mom says that's for people who need another kind of food. I couldn't eat it, or it would make me sick."

Erin rolled her eyes. "Are you allergic to something? It wouldn't make you sick unless you reacted to one of the ingredients."

"No. But she said it was only for sick people, and that if I ate it, I would get sick."

"Oh, I see. Well, I think she's mistaken about that, but she would know what makes you sick better than I would. It is for people who have celiac disease or some other sensitivity or allergy. But eating it wouldn't normally make you sick. You can eat rice and corn?"

"Yeah."

"Well, I use a lot of rice flour and corn starch, and alternative flours like that. It doesn't give you celiac disease. It just helps people who have celiac disease. Like Harold."

Eyes turned to Harold. Harold spread his hands apart. "I don't want to get sick, and she makes the best ever gluten-free baking. All of her stuff tastes just like it was made with regular wheat flour. Or better!"

Erin smiled. "Thank you for the endorsement, Harold. You are all welcome to come by the bakery when it is open. First customers always get a free cookie."

The way to a teenager's heart was his stomach, and the boys immediately exclaimed over the offer of a free cookie and high-fived each other. Erin smiled.

"Good, you all come by, then. I'll be looking for you."

She turned to find her car.

"I'll walk you to your car," Harold said importantly, striding forward to escort her.

"You don't need to do that. I'm not worried about the security of the parking lot. There's no one hanging around."

"You never know. I wouldn't want anything to happen to you. Then you wouldn't be able to make any more baking."

"Hey, yeah, that's right," the others agreed immediately, and suddenly Erin had an entire vanguard to walk her to her vehicle.

She laughed. "Well, thank you. You are all gentlemen."

"You have to be careful," Harold warned. "You know about all of the burglaries lately? Something could happen to you. We don't want that."

Erin slowed her pace a little, interested in hearing what he had to say. "It's just terrible about the burglaries, isn't it? Do you know some of the families that were affected?"

"Sure. Everyone goes to school here. And even if the families don't have teenagers, we still meet the little kids when we do mentoring or reading buddies. Or we go to church together."

"It's very sad for the little guys especially. You boys, you're almost grown up, so you could understand if your parents couldn't afford to replace the gifts that got stolen. But the little kids, how do you explain to them that Santa isn't coming this year?"

The boys looked at each other. They kicked rocks and elbowed each other as they walked across the parking lot. Erin drew her jacket to herself, feeling suddenly chilly.

"Do you know who the police are looking at?" Harold asked. "I know you and Officer Piper are..." he ducked his head, "you know, a couple... Do you know who they are investigating?"

Erin shook her head. "He hasn't said anything to me. He can't really talk to me about it. Why? Is there someone you think they should be looking at?"

Harold shrugged and looked at the other boys uncertainly. Erin waited to see if they had something to tell her. They dropped their gazes and didn't answer. They reached Erin's car. Erin unlocked it, then stood there, looking at them.

"Do you boys know something?"

"Maybe they should look at people from out of town," Connor Walker said finally. "People who come here to work over the Christmas season… you know… or who have just moved here recently."

"Not me!" Harold said hotly.

"Did I say you, man? I just mean, there are people that you can trust, and there are people who are outsiders… people who ain't from around here and aren't part of the community."

"I'm from Tennessee. My roots go back to these mountains."

Connor rolled his eyes dramatically. "I know, man. Just cool your jets. I'm saying *outsiders.*"

Erin looked at them, wondering, as Harold did, whether they considered her an outsider. She had been born in Tennessee and had lived there in her early years. But as far as any of the young people or those who hadn't known Clementine knew, she was an outsider too, someone who had just shown up in Bald Eagle Falls the previous year and didn't belong there. It took a lot longer than a year for the backwoods Tennesseans to recognize a person as one of their own. But Erin too had the pedigree to prove that she belonged there.

"Is there someone in particular you are thinking about?" she asked Connor.

The boy didn't seem to want to accuse anyone straight out. Erin thought about what he had said.

"Who would come to Bald Eagle Falls for work? It seems like there are enough people in Bald Eagle Falls who are looking for steady employment. It's pretty hard for us to support anyone from outside the community."

They nodded their agreement, faces grim. They had probably all felt the pinch of hard times. Erin studied them. The boys were tall and gangly, adolescent frames that hadn't yet filled out. Fourteen or fifteen years old, maybe. One of them had the shadow of a mustache above his lip. She didn't know any of them well except for Harold. Teenagers didn't come into the bakery very often. Mothers dragged the younger children in and out, but teenagers who were old enough to be left at home or to come and go on their own didn't make it into the bakery. Unless, like Harold, they wanted to grab a muffin between classes. And then they didn't talk to her, didn't identify themselves or tell her what family they belonged to. They just pointed or grunted what they wanted, tapped their bank cards or tossed a few bills on the counter, and were gone again before they could be missed at school.

"*Who* comes to Bald Eagle Falls to work?" Erin repeated.

She wanted an answer. She waited for them to either give in or to sneer at her and walk away. Harold seemed to be the thread holding them to her. He knew and trusted her, so they were willing to talk to her.

"Harold? Is there someone specific you are talking about? Who comes from outside to work in Bald Eagle Falls?"

"Just over the holiday season, you know? There are other jobs created around the holiday, and sometimes people come from out of town."

Erin looked at him.

"Like the Santas," the boy with the mustache contributed.

"The Santas?"

There were Santas. Erin hadn't stopped to think about where they had come from. She assumed that they were Bald Eagle Falls residents like everyone else. But they wore beards that obscured their faces, so she hadn't recognized them or even taken a second look at them. There were always Santas at Christmas. On the street corners ringing bells and collecting charitable donations. In the stores for children to tell their wishes to and to have pictures taken with to send to grandmas. She'd even seen one playing the violin on Main Street a few days before, busking for change.

"They come from outside Bald Eagle Falls?"

"Some of them," Harold agreed.

Erin pondered that and nodded slowly. They were anonymous, practically invisible. They could watch the shoppers coming and going and identify who might have a particularly good haul of electronics or higher-priced gifts. There could be a second person tailing such targets home to see where they lived so that their houses could be burgled later.

"I'll have to ask Officer Piper whether he is looking into them," she told the boys. "Is that what you want?"

They looked down at the ground and their feet and cast furtive glances at each other. They didn't want to tell her outright that they knew something, or to tell her whether they suspected someone. They wouldn't go to the police, and if questioned by the police would undoubtedly deny knowing anything at all about the thefts.

But she was sure they didn't want the burglar to get away. Didn't want him to keep ripping off the families in Bald Eagle Falls and making people unhappy. Especially the children. Especially if he wasn't even from Bald Eagle Falls.

Erin couldn't tell Terry that the boys thought it might be one of the Santas, but she could ask him if he was investigating them. Plant the seed. She wouldn't tell him she had gotten a tip, she would just let him consider the idea and then pursue it on his own.

Harold nodded at Erin, looking at her sideways as if he were embarrassed. "Yeah, maybe you could ask him that," he agreed.

One of the boys tapped the roof of Erin's car twice, and at that signal, they left her there and returned to the basketball court to resume their game.

CHAPTER 11

When Erin got back home, she was ready to cuddle on the couch with Terry for a few minutes to find out how his day had gone, and then to go to bed. It had been a long day and she just wanted to get to sleep.

But when she opened the front door, she could hear voices in the kitchen. She stopped for a moment and listened. It wasn't that she didn't often have people stopping in to visit, and Vic and Willie came and went as they pleased, but she hadn't been expecting anyone, and people generally knew that she retired to bed early and wasn't available to chat past the early evening.

She recognized Terry's voice, but not the other male voice that answered him. She listened for a moment, but couldn't make out their words to get a clue as to the visitor's identity.

But it was her own house. There was no point in waiting at the door or trying to hide or pretend she wasn't there. She walked into the living room and then through the doorway to the kitchen.

"Hi, I'm home."

Terry was leaning against the counter with a can of beer in his hand. He smiled a greeting and looked quickly at his watch. "I didn't realize it was that late. I'm sorry." He turned to his guest.

"Erin and I will want some time together before she has to go to bed, so…"

The other man was Stayner, the new deputy who had joined the police department temporarily to cover for Terry's position as he was recovering from his injuries. They had managed to find room in the budget to keep him on permanently as Terry transitioned back to work. Bald Eagle Falls had needed another deputy for some time. Terry had worked a lot of extra hours keeping the town safe and responding to calls. Having Stayner on permanently would allow them to split up the police work and let Terry work a more normal schedule.

Erin smiled and nodded to Stayner, but she wasn't exactly happy to see him there. He was very different from Terry. Not as experienced as Officer Piper, he tended to be a bit of a bully and to rush into things without thinking, assuming that he was always right and making snap judgments that may or may not be correct.

Terry thought that he would eventually wear down the rough edges and Stayner would become steadier and less inclined to make assumptions about people, but Erin wasn't sure it was a matter of his inexperience. It might just be his personality and would remain no matter what his training was.

"Hello, Officer Stayner. Nice to see you," she said politely. She didn't ask him how he was or what he was doing there. She didn't want a conversation with him. Terry had indicated it was time for him to go and Erin didn't want to delay his exit.

"Miss Price," Stayner acknowledged. "Hope you're having a good Christmas season."

Erin looked at Terry. He didn't correct Stayner and point out that Erin was an atheist and didn't observe the season. They just both looked at him.

"Just fine," Erin said finally, feeling that some response was necessary. "And you too, I hope."

"Well…" Stayner drawled the word out, "it's been an interesting one so far. I wasn't expecting quite so much action in Bald Eagle Falls. The theft of the donations for needy children has been a big deal. We're getting a lot of pressure from the community to figure out who stole the toys and is responsible for these burglaries. And they want it solved now, not after Christmas has come and gone."

"That makes sense," Erin agreed. "They all feel vulnerable. They don't want to think that they could have their Christmas stolen away too. Like in the movie."

Stayner looked at her blankly.

"The Dr. Seuss story," Erin clarified.

He still wasn't getting it. Erin cleared her throat uncomfortably.

"The Grinch," she said. "You know how in the Grinch story, he steals away everybody's presents, and trees, and turkeys, and decorations. Every last thing. And even though the people in Whoville still had Christmas and were happy about it, the people here are afraid that their families will be sad and the kids will be traumatized by Santa not bringing them presents this year... you know..."

Stayner nodded slowly. "The Grinch," he repeated.

Surely he had read the story or seen the cartoon or the motion picture. He hadn't lived under a rock. Everyone knew the storyline.

Stayner rubbed his chin, just starting to darken with five o'clock shadow. "Yes, I can understand the comparison," he agreed. "But this isn't a cartoon and people aren't going to get up in the morning and sing in delight if they discover all of their presents stolen."

"Exactly," Erin agreed. "That's just... a fairy tale and people know it. They know that their kids wouldn't be singing on Christmas morning if everything was gone. They'd be crying and complaining, and there would be nothing they could do about it."

"The police department is going to do a toy drive," Terry contributed. "We're going to try to replace as many of the stolen needy children's donations as we can. We might not be able to raise enough in the short time that we have, but we can try. We'll get more than if we don't do anything."

"That's good! I'm doing a bake sale too. And they're organizing some other fundraisers to try to help the families who have had their gifts stolen."

"Might do better collecting donations in the city," Stayner suggested. "They don't have the same connection with the families as Bald Eagle Falls residents do, but then we wouldn't be asking the same people to donate as who couldn't afford to get Christmas gifts in the first place. People are going to get tapped out pretty quickly, between their own Christmas donations and giving what they can to the fundraising efforts. Having ten different fundraisers isn't going to bring in any more money than two if people just don't have the money to give."

"Yeah," Erin agreed. "That's what I was thinking too. Now not only do people have to prepare for their own Christmases, but they have to do extra baking for the bake sale, then buy other people's baking when they don't need it; we're just adding to people's time and asking for more of their money."

"What we need to do is to find the burglars and put them behind bars, and to salvage what we can of whatever they haven't fenced. That's how we get people's' Christmases back."

Erin had to admit that his arguments made sense. But then, that was precisely what he said the people of Bald Eagle Falls were pressuring him to do. Get the burglaries solved, and do it before Christmas. It was a pretty tall order.

It didn't look like Stayner was heading out the door, despite Terry's comment that it was time for him to leave. He seemed instead to be settling into the conversation. Erin glanced at Terry to see if he were going to make another effort to kick Stayner out and, when he didn't, decided to ask her questions and go to bed whether Stayner was still there or not.

"Do you have any suspects?"

Terry pursed his lips and didn't answer. He was always careful about involving Erin in a case or giving her information that was not already public. Stayner didn't seem to have any such reservations.

"We have a few," he offered. "But if you're asking if we have any evidence as to who did it, that's another story. He has been pretty careful not to leave any fingerprints or other hard evidence for us to analyze."

"For burglaries, they've been remarkably clean," Terry agreed. "Very professional. And no broken doors or glass."

"Do you think they were let in? Or that they picked the locks?"

"Can't find anything to suggest that they were let in. The victims have been pretty broken up. I can't see any reason they would have been involved in the break-ins. It isn't like they are putting in huge insurance claims. They're pretty devastated. I don't think that any of the victims let them in."

"So they must have picked the locks."

Stayner nodded. "And the burglar alarms disarmed, if there are any."

Erin couldn't help looking at the control panel for her own burglar alarm. She'd had it bypassed once before, and didn't like to think that there was someone in town who had special expertise in getting around alarms.

Not that anyone would be targeting her. Anyone who knew anything about her would know that she wouldn't have any Christmas presents around or any pricey electronic equipment. She had a computer and a tablet and, of course, her phone, but she wasn't the type of person who bought high-end gadgetry. They were all budget purchases. Things that the boys playing basketball at the school would roll their eyes over.

"Are you looking at people from out of town?" She tried the question that the teenagers had suggested.

Stayner's brows drew down. "Out of town? It isn't like there are a lot of people here who are from out of town," he pointed out.

It wasn't until he said it in that defensive tone that Erin

thought about the fact that *he* was one of the most recent arrivals. Surely the teens hadn't thought that Stayner had anything to do with the burglaries…

Though, of course, he *would* have the professional skills needed.

"I just thought… there are a few people who aren't normally here, and maybe they could have been involved."

Stayner shook his head, scowling more deeply. "People here are so insular. They think that it couldn't be anyone they know. All of the crime must have been committed by an outsider."

"No…" He was uncomfortably close to the truth.

"You need to be thinking about some of your friends. William Andrews. Jeremy Jackson. These are men known to be involved in organized crime. They would be just the kind of people to be involved in something like this. Did you ever think of that?"

Erin took a moment to process his comment. Willie or Jeremy? She trusted them both completely. Or almost completely. In the past, she might have wondered whether they were involved in the goings-on in Bald Eagle Falls, but she knew them better now. She didn't believe that either of them would be stealing from the families of Bald Eagle Falls. Not from little children.

In her mind, she saw Willie's dark, stained face, and Jeremy's easy manner and wide grin. Jeremy was always up for anything, and she knew that he had lied to her in the past. And she'd caught him with a bump key which he had used to unlock her door. Could he be supplementing his income through burglary?

And Willie, though he had always treated Erin with kindness and consideration, was involved in all kinds of schemes. Were all of them legal? Terry had often expressed suspicions about Willie's sense of morality. They knew he had worked for five years as a soldier for the Dyson clan. He would have all of the knowledge and training needed for something like the Grinch burglaries.

But would he do something like that? If he saw it as a source of easy income and wanted to supplement what he was making with other ventures?

"It couldn't be either of them…" she murmured in protest.

"Oh, couldn't it?" Stayner challenged. "They don't have solid alibis. You have no idea what they might have been doing at night when you thought they were home in bed. No one can know."

"Well, they have partners. They're not sleeping alone."

Stayner gave a shrug. Erin tried to read his expression. Did he think that the men had snuck out at night without their bedmates knowing about it?

"You don't think that Beaver and Vic are involved too, do you? Beaver is a federal agent!"

"It wouldn't be the first time that a federal agent broke the law or had a… sideline."

"Beaver would never do something like that!"

"You don't know her that well," Stayner challenged. "And even if you think you do, she is trained in deception, in pretending to be something other than she is. So what makes you think that you would know anything about her true personality and motivation?"

Erin stared at him. Erin knew the showy Beaver, the one who made a point of facing off against a drug dealer after rear-ending his car in the middle of Main Street. She knew the Beaver who joked about anything serious and made fun of herself with self-deprecating wit. She had been with Beaver when she was off duty, when her guard was down. And she had seen Beaver relaxed and knew her dry sense of humor and the loyalty she had for her friends. She knew the Beaver who was anxious about Jeremy or Campbell Cox.

But maybe all of those were fronts. Perhaps *none* of them was the real Beaver.

Erin shook her head. "I know Beaver. And Willie too. They wouldn't do anything to hurt a child. Neither one of them would."

"No child has been hurt. It doesn't injure a child or even traumatize them not to get a Christmas present. So they have a quiet Christmas with their family at home and don't get to open a present. How is that going to hurt them?"

"It does. I know what that's like."

Stayner stared at her for a moment, not blinking, then slowly nodded his head. He looked at Terry, who didn't say what he thought of Beaver and Willie or whether the burglar had done anything to hurt anyone.

Terry looked again at his watch. "I'll see you tomorrow, Rod."

Stayner took the hint this time. He shrugged dramatically and headed toward Erin and the kitchen door. Erin stepped back out of his way. He didn't pause or give her any extra space, just barreled by as if she weren't there.

"I'll see you again, Miss Price," he said gruffly.

Erin didn't answer. She watched him leave through the front door. Terry followed and locked the door and armed the burglar alarm.

"Sorry. He was supposed to be gone by the time you got home. Are you okay?"

"Sure." Erin rubbed her eyes tiredly. "I'm fine. He's… you don't believe that Willie or Beaver was involved in these burglaries, do you? That's ridiculous."

"Unfortunately, it's not as ridiculous as you would like to think. I can't talk to you about the details of an investigation. I wouldn't have said as much as he did, but that was his choice."

"You don't think that Beaver could have anything to do with the burglaries."

"What I think doesn't have anything to do with the investigation. That's not my judgment to make. I have to investigate anyone who is identified as a suspect. And as Officer Stayner says… it is possible to get around their alibis."

"But you can say the same thing about anyone. Most of the population would have been sleeping when the burglaries happened. So how could anyone prove that they were in bed asleep when everyone else was in bed asleep?"

"Some people don't sleep soundly enough for their partner to sneak out. But again, how do you prove that? Establishing alibis is only one part of the process. We will be investigating motives, where the suspects were at the time of each of the burglaries, not just one. If they have been seen doing anything suspicious, making unusual purchases, or seem to have more money or high-priced items than normal. Investigating."

"But you don't think it's either of them."

Terry didn't move or speak for a minute, his lips pressed together in a thin line as he considered his answer. After a while, he shook his head. "No. I don't think it's Willie or Beaver. But that's a gut feeling, a feeling that I have because they are our friends. I can't go by that. I have to remain unbiased."

"I know." Erin took a couple of steps to close the space between them and wrapped her arms around Terry. She was glad to know his opinion, even if he weren't allowed to rely on his feelings. He didn't think it was Beaver or Willie either. And he had to be right. He was a good cop.

"You need to go to bed," Terry said, rubbing her back in firm, soothing circles. "You must be exhausted."

"I am. Or I was. I'm not sure I am anymore." The discussion with Stayner had gotten her wound up. She wasn't sure she was going to be able to quiet her brain if she went straight to bed. "Maybe we can have a cup of tea and relax for a few minutes first."

"Sure." He kissed her forehead gently. "Why don't you get your jammies on and I'll start the tea?"

He wasn't much of a cook, but he was certainly qualified to start the water heating. "Thanks. That sounds really nice."

CHAPTER 12

*E*rin was clumsy in her morning duties and nothing seemed to be coming together the way it was supposed to. Erin had been working at the bakery for long enough that her hands knew what to do without her brain, yet she just couldn't seem to get it together.

"You look tired," Vic commented.

"I am tired, I guess."

"Get to bed late last night? How long did that school meeting go? I'm sorry I didn't get there, but Willie and I had some errands to run in the city, and they really couldn't wait."

"No need for both of us to be there. I don't think you would have provided any additional benefit. You might as well have gotten done what you needed to."

"I guess. But I don't like to see you having to take everything on. How did it go?"

"Fine." Erin stifled a yawn. "It didn't really run that late, but then when I got home, Officer Stayner was talking with Terry, and then I couldn't settle down right away…"

Vic made a sympathetic noise. "You should have said something. We could call someone else in. We have enough people on staff now that you don't need to take it all on yourself, you know."

"I'm not. And I wouldn't have been able to sleep late anyway. Once I hit my usual wake-up time, my body is just too disrupted to get any more rest. I might as well be up and baking."

She bent down to get a better look at the batter the mixer was swirling around and banged her head on the arm of the mixer.

"Oof. Okay, maybe there are some things I shouldn't be doing." Erin rubbed the spot she had hit. "Ouch. That hurt."

Vic was trying to suppress her giggles but wasn't having much success. "I'm sorry! I'm not laughing at you. Really."

"You're laughing with me."

"Exactly."

"I'm not making change today. You'd better be on the till."

"I think so, or we might be bankrupt by the end of the day."

They worked together in silence for a while.

"We're supposed to be making extra cookies for this bake sale thing?" Vic inquired.

"Yes. A few dozen should do it. I'm thinking of doing more Grinch cookies, packaging them individually. Buy a Grinch to fight the Grinch."

"Oooh, good idea."

"I don't know how much money it is going to bring in, though. It's like Officer Stayner was saying last night. People don't have the money. It isn't that we need to be clever and think up more ways to persuade them to give. They just don't have the money. It doesn't matter whether it is a cookie or a book."

"Well... we'll pray it's enough."

Mary Lou Cox was by for her baking that afternoon. Erin smiled, happy to see that the neat, trim woman with ash-blond hair was out and about and looking like herself. She had been very worried about Mary Lou since her son had been arrested at Thanksgiving dinner for possession of illegal drugs. It had not been an easy time for her, even when they had managed to prove that the drugs had been planted in Campbell's car. Some people would always believe the bad about people. Even if their opinion was proven wrong, they could never quite let it go.

"Hi, Mary Lou. How is it going?"

Mary Lou smiled and smoothed her pantsuit. "I'm well, Erin." She hesitated before offering, "You're looking a little worn."

"Oh, does it show?" Erin rubbed her eyes, hoping to erase any trace of puffiness.

"Have you been doing too much? With Christmas coming, you must be very busy with your baking."

"Yes, it's busy. And I don't always sleep the best. But it's been manageable." She stifled a yawn. That was the trouble with thinking about being tired. Just the suggestion was enough to make her start yawning. "I was just up a little late last night. We had that meeting at the school…" Erin had seen Mary Lou there, but had not stopped to talk to her. Mary Lou had seemed occupied in discussions with others, and Erin had been impatient to get home, not realizing she would end up not being able to sleep anyway.

"Of course," Mary Lou agreed. "It was nice of you to volunteer for the bake sale."

"Well, I didn't exactly, but it was fine. I guess I'm the most obvious choice."

"Volunteering at the school isn't like volunteering in other places," Vic put in. "If you don't object loudly enough, you just accepted."

"Yes, that's exactly what happened." Erin laughed. "I was volun-told."

"If it is too much, then you can say so," Mary Lou advised. "People do drop out of assignments."

"I'll manage. We're going to do some Grinch cookies. You know, so people can help fight off the Grinch."

"That's clever. You always have such interesting ideas."

Erin wasn't sure it was a compliment. *Interesting* ideas rather than good ideas.

"How are you guys doing?" she asked. "And how's Campbell?"

"We're hanging in there. Campbell will be home for Christmas… I don't know for how long, but…" She shrugged, trying to look like it didn't matter to her. Of course it did. She would want Cam to spend at least a few days home. Since his arrest had ruined their Thanksgiving, it was only right that he try to make it up by spending some quality time with his mother and brother. And they would, Erin assumed, make some time to visit Roger in the facility where he was incarcerated.

"And Josh…?"

"He's still in school, that's about all I can say. He doesn't say much to me about how he is doing. I haven't had calls from the school saying that he's failing or missing classes. But he's not doing any of the things he used to do, the sports and after-school activities. He doesn't bring friends home. I don't know who he's spending time with at school, if anyone."

Josh had seemed like such an honest and caring person when Vic and Erin had spent time with him in the city. It was hard to believe, with his level of maturity, that he was still a teenager. The two boys had been through a lot in their young lives, and it showed in the way they behaved, Campbell falling apart and abandoning his old life for something fleeting and uncertain in the city, and Joshua trying the best he could to keep it together, but clearly struggling. He wanted his brother to come back, or at least to know that he was safe. And he tried to protect his mother and not make her unhappy. But he couldn't keep doing everything he had previously, being an all-star and honor student and working to contribute to the family income.

"I wish I could help," she told Mary Lou. "He seems like such a great kid."

The lines in Mary Lou's face softened. "He really is," she agreed. "He's not perfect. None of us is. He's no angel. But he's a good kid, caring kid, and I hate to see him drifting."

Erin decided she would try to talk to Joshua. Maybe there was something she could do or say that would make a difference. Or perhaps she could ask Beaver for suggestions. Beaver had been in contact with Cam, and she'd talked to both boys after the ill-fated trip to the city, so maybe she would have some insight into the best way to help Josh.

"At least he's still in school. You don't have to worry about where he is or what he's doing during school hours."

Mary Lou sighed. "Hopefully. You never know how well they are keeping track of the kids. Not all of the teachers take attendance regularly."

"I'm sure you'd hear about it from someone if he was getting into trouble."

CHAPTER 13

*E*rin arrived home and tiredly put down her purse and greeted Terry. K9 jumped to his feet to nose at her hand and get ear scratches, and Marshmallow hopped over to get his share as well. Erin frowned, looking around.

"Where's the other critter? Is Blossom pouting because of K9?"

Terry looked around, thinking about it. "I haven't seen much of him today. He was yowling this morning, but he must be in the bedroom sleeping, I think."

It was unusual for Orange Blossom not to meet her at the door unless he was upset about something. Erin tried to think of what it might be as she walked down the hall to the bedroom and peeked in, expecting to see him sleeping on mussed-up blankets on her bed. But he wasn't there. She looked around the room and under the bed.

"Terry? He didn't get out, did he? I don't see him."

"I haven't been out or had the door open. He has to be here somewhere."

Erin looked under the bed again with her phone switched to flashlight mode, just in case she had missed him. But he wasn't there. She checked the closet in case he had been shut in there. Then she headed for the bathroom. Blossom had shut himself in there before, and Terry might not have noticed the reason for his meowing to be let out, thinking he was just being vocal.

But the bathroom door was open a crack. Erin glanced in and didn't see him there.

A search of the rest of the house and calling to him turned up no results. Erin returned to the bathroom to check it again, and realized that her furry friend was hunched up behind the commode.

"Terry? There's something wrong."

Erin made calling noises to Orange Blossom and put out her hand, expecting him to come to her. But he just looked at her with glazed eyes and didn't move. Erin dragged him out.

"Oh, Blossom. What's wrong? What's wrong, baby, huh?"

She petted his too-dry fur and examined his face, mouth, and belly, looking for any sign of what was wrong. He had feces caked on his backside, and just lay there listlessly as she poked and prodded him.

Terry appeared in the doorway. He immediately looked concerned.

"What's wrong?" he asked, kneeling down and squeezing in beside her.

"I don't know. He's sick. How long has he been like this?"

"I haven't seen him most of the day. He was okay when you left, wasn't he?"

"Yes, everything was normal this morning."

Terry did an examination similar to Erin's, but she was more confident in his. He had grown up around cats and other animals and she had not.

"Wrap him up in a towel and let's get him over to Doc's."

"He'll be closed."

"I'll call him. Get Blossom ready to go."

"Okay."

He got up. With tears in her eyes, Erin pulled one of the towels down from the rod beside her and carefully wrapped the cat up like a burrito. He didn't struggle and only made one low moan of protest. For a cat who was usually so loud, his silence was the scariest part.

She could hear Terry making a phone call. By the time she got to the door, he was hanging up. He scooped up her purse and led the way out to the car.

"I'm so sorry, Erin. I should have noticed that something was wrong. It didn't even occur to me that he hadn't been underfoot all day."

"It's not your fault. I'm his owner, I should have known he was sick. What do you think it is? He hasn't been around any other cats to catch something. I couldn't see any injuries. Cats don't just get sick for no reason, do they?"

"They can get sick just like any other animals. Just pray it's nothing serious. Doc will sort him out."

In a few minutes, they were at the vet's office. Doctor Edmunds was there to let them in. He looked at Orange Blossom's face sticking out the end of the towel wrap and led the way to one of the examination rooms.

"Bring him right here. Let's have a look at this little fellow and see what's wrong."

Erin put her bundle down on the examining table. Orange Blossom felt light and frail.

The doctor unwrapped the towel and began his examination, palpating the cat's stomach, using his stethoscope to listen to his heart and respiration. He checked Blossom's eyes, ears, and mouth, and used some wipes to clean off the cat's backside and check for problems there. Erin watched anxiously, waiting for his diagnosis.

"Has he been outside?" Doc asked.

"No, not lately. I take him out sometimes just into the yard, but he hasn't been out for a few days. He hasn't been around any other animals, just Marshmallow and K9."

Doc's eyes went to the open examination room door, where he could see Terry and K9 waiting. "K9 looks like he's fine."

"Yes. He and Marshmallow both seem perfectly normal."

"Has he changed his diet? Litter box habits?"

"I didn't know anything was wrong until I got home from work. That's the first sign that he was sick. He was okay this morning."

"Energetic this morning?"

"Yeah. He was just the same as any other morning. Talkative, playful, demanding to be fed."

He nodded. He petted Orange Blossom gently as they talked. "Could he have gotten into household cleaners, antifreeze, weed killer, or rodent poison?"

Erin shook her head. She was always careful to put such things out of reach. "No, I don't think so."

"You're a baker."

"Yes."

"But you probably don't do much baking at home, just at the bakery?"

"I experiment at home, developing new recipes."

"Could he have gotten into chocolate or another baking ingredient?"

Erin hesitated. While she didn't feed him people food other than a bit of whatever meat she was cooking, she never worried too much about him eating something that had fallen to the floor, and more than once had found him nosing around in the pantry between meals.

"It's possible. I didn't see anything he'd gotten into, but I rushed him straight over here without checking the kitchen or pantry."

"Let me know after you go home if you can tell what he might have eaten. I'll treat him the best I can, give him fluids and try to neutralize whatever might still be in his digestive tract, though it looks like whatever it was has probably already moved through and he's absorbed whatever toxins were present." He stroked Blossom's head. "His heartbeat is still strong, but he's feeling pretty rotten. This is probably as bad as he'll get, but we'll keep an eye on him and do whatever we can to help him recover."

Erin nodded, her eyes brimming with tears.

"Now, I can do some tests on liver and kidney function, but unless you're willing to do dialysis or other extreme measures, that's just an extra expense."

Erin swallowed. "Let's see how he does before spending a whole lot." It was not an easy decision to make. She wasn't sure whether it was the right one. Should she do everything she could no matter what the cost?

The vet nodded his agreement. "Okay. Why don't you say goodbye to him for now, and I'll take him back and get an IV going. Just getting fluids into him will make a big difference, he's quite dehydrated right now."

Erin bent down over Orange Blossom, giving him a gentle hug and snuggle and kissing the top of his head. "I'm sorry I have to leave you, buddy, but the doctor is going to help you to feel better." She scratched his ears and chin and gave him one final pet. "Okay," she told Doc Edmunds.

He scooped Orange Blossom up and held him cuddled against his body. "We'll take good care of him, mom. I'll give you a call in the morning to let you know how he's doing."

Erin returned to Terry, tears spilling down her cheeks.

CHAPTER 14

Vic walked into the kitchen in her usual familiar manner, already chattering about something she had heard or maybe something about what she and Willie had done the night before. She got a good look at Erin and stopped mid-sentence.

"Erin? What's wrong?"

"It's Orange Blossom."

Vic immediately cast her eyes around and, not seeing the cat, looked back at Erin, her face pale and mouth partly open. "What happened? Did he get out?"

"He's sick. Terry and I took him to the vet last night. I won't know how he's doing until later this morning." Erin sniffled. "It's just really hard to wait."

"Sick? Sick how?"

"Doc thinks maybe he got into something. Chocolate or a household chemical. But I'm pretty careful about things like that. He might have gotten into something in the pantry, but I don't see anything spilled or knocked over. Nothing that he's gotten into. Maybe I let him eat something that had fallen to the floor while I was baking and it ended up making him sick..."

"Oh, honey!" Vic stepped forward and enfolded Erin in a soft hug. "Hey, It's not your fault. Don't blame yourself. You know how cats are; they're curious about everything. They get into things. He'll be okay, won't he? What did Doc say?"

"He thought Blossom would get better. He was really dehydrated, Doc was going to give him an IV and wait and see…"

Vic released Erin and patted her on the back. "I'm sure he'll be okay. They'll have him fixed up in no time. I'm so sorry, I didn't know he was sick."

Erin forced a smile. "Yes, he'll get better. I'm sure everything will be fine."

~

Erin was keeping a close watch on the clock as she worked at Auntie Clem's. What time would Doc be at the clinic and call her back? Eight o'clock? Nine? If there were an emergency or a desperate case, he might forget to even call her.

At least if he didn't call her, that at least would suggest that Orange Blossom was doing well. If he were in dire straits, Doc wouldn't forget to call her with an update.

Vic noticed Erin's frequent looks at the clock, but just raised an eyebrow and didn't make any comment.

Finally, at about five minutes past nine, Erin's phone vibrated. She pulled it out and looked at the face.

Veterinary clinic.

Erin swiped to answer the call and held it up to her ear. "Hello?"

"Miss Price, Doc Edmunds here. Did you get any sleep last night?"

"Not much," Erin admitted. "I was pretty anxious."

"Well, your little friend is feeling a lot better this morning. Not one hundred percent; I'd still like to keep an eye on him until at least the end of the day, but I am encouraged."

"Oh, good." Erin blew her breath out and gave Vic a thumbs up. "Thank goodness for that. So you think he'll be okay?"

"It's quite an improvement over last night. I'd like to see him eating and having normal elimination to show that everything is in working order. Then the best thing for him will be to be back home in his familiar environment."

"Maybe tonight?"

"Hopefully, yes."

"I'm so glad! Thank you for calling me."

"All right. We'll talk later. Give me a call when you're getting off work."

The day had dragged on incredibly long. Erin had felt like she would never get to the end of it. They managed to get the last few customers out of the bakery a little before the time that they would normally close, flipped the sign over to 'closed,' and did their usual tidying up and preparation for the next day. Erin felt like she was fumbling with everything instead of working smoothly as she normally did. She just wanted to be out of there and to get to the vet's to see Orange Blossom.

"We can probably leave it at that," Vic said, looking around. "If there's anything else, we can catch it up tomorrow."

"I don't know, I should probably…" Erin trailed off. She wasn't getting done the tasks that she knew she needed to get done; what was she doing trying to add to the list? Vic was right. Everything else could wait. They had the essentials done. "Okay. Let's go."

Vic smiled. They gathered their purses, phones, and keys, and headed for the door. Erin hit the crash bar on the back door and, when she reached the car, looked back to see where Vic was. Vic came through the door shaking her head.

"What is it?" Erin asked.

"Just arming the burglar alarm, boss."

The blood rushed to Erin's face as she looked back and realized she'd just bolted out of the bakery without even thinking of the burglar alarm. "You'd think that after all that has happened around here, I would remember about the security!"

"Your mind is on other things right now. It's called mommy brain."

"Well… I'm not sure if I can claim that, but I certainly am worried about my 'baby.'"

It was a good thing that they didn't have far to go to get to the vet's. Erin was rattled by forgetting to arm the burglar alarm, and kept making simple mistakes in operating her car, which she'd had for three years, so it wasn't like she didn't know how to drive it. She hit the windshield wipers instead of the turn signal, hit the brakes too hard, and was generally jittery. Vic didn't say anything about it, but Erin was sure she was wondering if her boss were losing her mind.

They pulled into the empty parking lot and Erin urged the car gently into a parking space and shifted it into park.

"He knows you're coming, right?" Vic asked. "He was going to wait for you?"

"Yes. It's closed, but he said he'd be here waiting for me."

They approached the doors and found them still unlocked. Doc Edmunds strolled into the reception area when he heard the door, and smiled at Erin.

"Right on time, Miss Price. Ready for your furry friend?"

"Am I ever! I've been on pins and needles all day. Or is it on tenterhooks? I can never remember which is right."

He chuckled and motioned her into the same examination room that she had taken Orange Blossom into the day before.

Blossom was already there, lying on a clean towel, curled up in a ball. At Erin's entrance, his head popped up and he looked at her with an expression of affront. Erin didn't know if he was upset because she had awakened him, or because she had left him there all day. He certainly did appear to have his nose out of joint.

"Hey, Blossom! How are you doing? Are you feeling better?" She petted him and gave him a gentle hug. "Are you ready to go home?"

He let out a groan that sounded like an old man's, then slowly straightened his body until it was all in a line. He stretched his hind legs out and spread his toes, a shudder running through his body as he got everything ready to go. Erin bent over and kissed him on the top of the head.

"It's good to see you looking normal again." She looked over at Doc. "Though, he'd normally be scolding me and pacing, yowling to go home."

"Yes, he's not one hundred percent, but he's on the mend. He'll probably sleep a lot over the next few days and not have all of his usual energy for a while yet. He needs a chance to recover. But he can do that at home and doesn't need to stay here."

"Good. Thank you so much for helping him. I don't know what I would have done if..." She couldn't even finish the thought out loud. She'd grown very attached to her furry baby.

Blossom pawed at Erin, then reached up and put both of his front paws onto Erin's chest, standing up tall to bump her with the top of his head. Erin scratched his ears.

"Yeah, good to see you too. Shall we go home?"

He allowed Erin to pick him up and cuddled against her. Erin looked at the vet. "What do I owe you?"

"I'll email you and you can e-transfer. Sarah has gone home, and I always mess up with the point-of-sale machine."

"Okay, thanks."

"I sent some samples off to the lab to see if we can identify what he ate. You didn't discover anything that he had gotten into?"

"No, I checked the pantry and everywhere else I could think of, but I couldn't find anything open or spilled. I don't know what it could have been."

"We may find out, or we may not. It will be a while before the results come back."

"Okay. Let me know... I'll get rid of it, whatever it is."

"Of course."

Erin and Vic walked back out to the car. Orange Blossom

looked around, but didn't struggle or make any attempt to jump out of Erin's arms. He seemed completely content to stay with her, wherever she was going.

Once in the car, though, Vic held her arms out. "You can't drive with him in your lap. Give him here."

Erin reluctantly relinquished the cat to her friend.

"It's only for a few minutes, and then you can have him back again."

"I know." Erin concentrated on driving, even though tears were blurring her vision. She'd been doing too much crying lately, and it bothered her. Vic either didn't notice, or didn't see the need to draw attention to the fact.

Then they were home. Erin gathered Orange Blossom back up in her arms and took him into the house. The cat kicked to be free as soon as she got him into the house, unlike his sedate behavior at the vet's office. Erin released him, putting him down on the floor.

He immediately started sniffing around to make sure that everything was as it should be and that she hadn't moved furniture or gotten a new cat while he was gone. Marshmallow hopped over to smell him and Orange Blossom gave him a few licks, something that he rarely did.

"Yeah, we're glad you're home," Erin murmured. "So glad that you're feeling better."

CHAPTER 15

Erin stopped at the grocery store to pick up a few necessities for the next batch of Christmas treats. It was bustling with shoppers and energy; she could feel the excitement of the holiday building as people tried to get everything together that they would need for their Christmas celebrations.

There were Christmas decorations up at the store. Garlands around the checkout stand poles, painted windows, and various other little touches that Erin knew she wouldn't see at one of the grocery stores in the city. It was nice to be in a small town. They really did go all out to make it nice for people.

As she waited for the cashier to check her items through the checkout, Erin's eyes landed on a Santa outside the store. The beard and body suit obscured the man's identity. She didn't know whether it was someone she knew or not. It would be pretty easy to get around town without anyone ever knowing who you really were in an outfit like that. She watched the man ringing his bell for donations. He watched the people coming out of the store, wishing them a Merry Christmas and angling for a donation to his pot.

Did he seem just a little too interested in what was in people's carts? Was he looking for some high-priced items that would be worthwhile stealing later?

Erin shook the thought off. People coming out of the grocery store? It wasn't like they were buying electronics or expensive children's toys, clothing, or jewelry at the grocery store. They were buying food. Turkey, stuffing, potatoes, and whatever else they wanted for their tables this year. And even though she called the burglar a Grinch, she didn't think he was actually interested in stealing every vestige of the Christmas spirit. He only wanted the high-value stuff.

"Erin?"

"Hmm?" Erin realized that the cashier was waiting for her. "Oh, sorry. Lost in my own little world. Who is your Santa this year?" She entered her PIN on the keypad.

The cashier looked out the front window. "He's not actually one of ours. Salvation Army, I think. They have them everywhere, you know."

"But he's on your property."

"No one minds. They can pretty much set up where they want. I know there are rules about business licenses and busking and all that, and where you are allowed to ply your trade, but it's for charity. Nobody really cares where the Santas set up at Christmas."

Erin nodded absently, thinking it through. She put her packed groceries into the shopping cart and pushed it out the doors, keeping an eye on the Santa.

She couldn't see his face well behind the beard, but he seemed to be a fairly young man. He gave her a hearty 'Merry Christmas' and rang his bell, watching to see if she would donate. Erin slowly took out her wallet, examining him.

"Who's under there?" she asked him. "Do I know you?"

"No ma'am." He took a step to the side to allow her to reach the donation pot, but she thought he was also doing it to distance himself from her. "I'm not from around here."

"Oh… do you do this every year, or…?"

He 'Merry Christmas-ed' a couple of other shoppers, shooting Erin an irritated look. "Times are tough. I'll take work wherever I can get it."

Erin nodded sympathetically. "Do you have a family?"

"I'm just trying to work, here, ma'am."

"I just thought maybe…" Erin pulled another bill from her wallet and held it out to him. "For you. For your little one."

He stood frozen for a moment, looking at her. "We're not allowed to take tips. All donations have to go into the pot."

But he reached his hand out, fingertips extending toward the cash.

"I already put money in the pot," Erin said. "You're not taking from the Salvation Army. This is for you and your family."

He took it from her, shoving it into his pocket and glancing around to see if anyone was watching.

"It's so sad," Erin said, "about all of the burglaries, isn't it? I feel bad for those families."

"Burglaries?"

"Our Grinch," Erin said, forcing a little laugh. "Stealing Christmas presents from families around here and from the needy children's collection."

He poked at his pocket, making sure that the money was going to stay there and was out of sight. "I don't know anything about that. I drive in, I do my bit, and drive home."

"Oh. Right." Erin couldn't see any way to draw the conversation out any further, and started to push her cart toward her car. "Well, Merry Christmas. I hope you make enough to have a nice time with your family."

"Merry Christmas," he repeated. He turned away from her and rang his bell vigorously at the next person coming out the doors.

Erin packed her groceries thoughtfully into her car.

How would anyone from out of town know which houses to

hit and when? Whoever had been stealing from families appeared to have known their schedules. They hadn't just been crimes of opportunity; they had been carefully planned. She couldn't see how someone from out of town would be able to do that. Unless they had an accomplice inside Bald Eagle Falls to feed them information.

It was a few days before Erin saw Beaver. A few days and a couple more burglaries later. Terry's mood was not good; the police department wasn't getting much further ahead on the case. He was getting dark circles around his eyes, and his answers when Erin tried to engage him in conversation were getting more terse.

Erin and Vic had Saturday off and had made arrangements for morning brunch with Beaver at the family restaurant. The restaurant always put on a nice brunch buffet. It was a more relaxed morning than Erin was used to, a nice break from her usually busy pace.

Vic looked from her plate with an eggwhite omelet, one buttermilk pancake, and berries, to Beaver's plate heaped with food, and shook her head.

"Where do you put it all?"

"I'm a very active person," Beaver said with a wide grin.

"Wow. You must be, to burn all of that off."

"It's also probably the only real meal that I'll have today. Jeremy is off doing his thing, and when I'm on my own, I tend just to graze. There's not much around the apartment. I'll pick up some fruit and granola bars, and that will do me the rest of the day."

Vic nodded.

Beaver turned to Erin. "So how is the investigation going?"

"What?" Erin was momentarily confused. She wasn't investigating anything.

"The Grinch. Have the boys in blue made any progress?"

"Not much," Erin admitted. "Not that Terry would tell me about it if they had; it's not any of my business. But from his mood… no, they're not getting anywhere."

Beaver started to work her way through her heaping plate of food. She chewed thoughtfully.

"There have been daytime burglaries as well as the evening break-ins. That says something about the burglar."

Erin considered. "Not someone who works all day."

"I would say not. Of course, it could be someone on shift work who is off some mornings, or someone could call in sick in order to commit a burglary. But my gut says not. This is someone who only works sporadically, if at all."

"That narrows it down a bit." Erin didn't say anything to Beaver about her being a suspect. Or Jeremy or Willie. Other people in Bald Eagle Falls fit the profile. Or it could be someone from outside of Bald Eagle Falls or someone who had just arrived recently. She didn't like to consider the possibility of one of her friends being involved. "What about someone like… someone who is just visiting Bald Eagle Falls? Someone who got some seasonal work for Christmas. Maybe a retail store or Santa Claus or Salvation Army."

"Possibly, but I think that's less likely. A stranger would be noticed. You are looking for someone who knows people's habits —when they are likely to be home or away. Someone who would know about the charity toy drive and where the donated items were kept. Someone new in town or visiting… I can't see that working."

"Unless he also has a Bald Eagle Falls contact," Vic suggested. "Someone who could give him that information."

Both of these conclusions matched Erin's thoughts on the subject.

"Right," Beaver agreed. "That would, of course, be a possibility as well. We may be looking at a group of perpetrators." She ate some more, then tapped her fork on the table as she thought. "A group of people would be a real possibility, based on the facts that I'm aware of."

"Do you want to suggest it to Terry?" Erin asked. "If I say something about it, he's going to think that I'm sticking my nose where it doesn't belong."

"And he won't think that about me?" Beaver asked with a chuckle.

"Well, at least you're law enforcement. I'm not, and he always gets irritated about me getting mixed up in things that the police are supposed to be investigating. And besides—you don't live with him."

"No, thank goodness."

Erin raised her eyebrows. "What is that supposed to mean? You like Terry."

"Officer Piper does a fine job. He is very conscientious. But he's not my type."

The comments that other women in Bald Eagle Falls usually made about Terry were envious comments about his good looks and how admired he was in the community. And then there was K9. The combination of a handsome officer in uniform and his cuddly-looking companion was enough to set most of the women swooning. They all told her how lucky she was. It was startling to hear a dissenting opinion.

"Too old for you?" Vic suggested to Beaver.

Her question made Erin wince. While Vic had not said much about it, Erin suspected that she had some issues with the older woman dating Vic's brother. Though Vic couldn't really object, considering that the disparity between her age and Willie's was considerably greater than that between Beaver and Jeremy. But dating an older woman was still not quite as acceptable in society as dating an older man, at least not in rural Tennessee.

Beaver was unfazed by Vic's comment. She smiled her usual wide, lazy grin, looking Vic in the eye. "No reason I have to date someone my age, is there, Miss Victoria?"

"No, of course not. I'm just wondering what you have against Terry. Most women in Bald Eagle Falls think he's a pretty good catch."

"I'm not most women. He's fine for someone like Erin, but I prefer someone a little less… uptight."

Erin bit the inside of her cheek to keep from responding. She paid close attention to her brunch. She couldn't deny the fact that Terry was strait-laced. She still didn't feel comfortable talking with him about everything that had happened in her life before moving to Bald Eagle Falls. There were a lot of things in her past that he probably wouldn't approve of. He knew some details of her former life from his previous investigations, but she had kept others to herself.

She cleared her throat and decided it was a good time to change the subject. "Hey, have you talked to Joshua Cox lately? I haven't seen him since… the thing in the city… and I was wondering if you'd had anything to do with him."

"Why?" Beaver asked baldly.

"Well… I worry about him. He's a nice kid, but I worry about what's going to happen without Campbell around, and with all of the stress on the family. Mary Lou worries so much about those boys…"

"Maybe it is time for her to let go and give them a bit more independence."

"She has… but that doesn't stop her from worrying."

"Or you, apparently. Or is this just Mary Lou's roundabout way of getting to me?"

"No. She doesn't know I'm asking. I didn't know whether

you'd had anything more to do with Joshua. So I thought…
there's no harm in asking."

"From what I can tell, Joshua is fine. He doesn't say much
about his personal life. I don't imagine he is enjoying school, but
what teenage boy does?"

Erin sighed. "Do you think I should talk to him? Maybe he'd
tell me…"

"What would he tell you? Everything that's wrong with his
life? I'm not sure why he would tell you that, unless you have
some connection with him that I'm not aware of."

"No."

Vic studied Beaver. "Is Joshua doing work for you, like Campbell? Is he an informant?"

"I wouldn't tell you if he was."

"I guess not." Vic laughed. "You wouldn't be much of a
handler if you did."

"I suggest you leave the Cox boys alone," Beaver told Erin.
"They don't need another parent."

CHAPTER 17

*E*rin headed over to the school to meet with Vice Principal Fitzroy to report on the progress of the bake sale and coordinate timing. She checked in at the office and was directed to a meeting room where Fitzroy was to join her. Erin looked around at the room. Lots of posters on the walls addressing teen social problems, just like in the classroom she had attended at the first time.

Before Fitzroy put in an appearance, Coach Hadrian stuck his head in the door. "Hey, Miss Price, I heard you were here. How's everything coming together for the bake sale?"

"It's coming. I talked to your wife the other day, and she's making those banana loaves like you said she would. We're very grateful for all of the support the bake sale is getting. I think it's going to be very nice. As long as there are as many people to buy the food as there are to make it."

"We usually have a pretty good response to fundraisers. I'm sure we'll have enough people."

Erin cast about for something else to talk with the coach about. "And... how are your teams doing? I didn't get a chance to ask you the other night. Do they play against teams in other towns, or just internally?"

"Most of the year we're just playing intramurals. But toward the end of the season, we'll join in some tournaments."

"So you're not doing that yet…. do you have good teams this year?" Erin looked toward the door to see if the vice principal were there yet. He had arranged for the time to meet, so he should have been there on time.

"They're pretty good. We've lost a few players since last year, so they'll have to play hard to make up for it."

"Do you know Joshua Cox? And his brother?"

"Yes. They were good players. I've talked to Josh a few times to try to convince him to play. I don't know why he had to drop the teams. He wasn't as good at sports as Campbell, but we're still missing him."

"Maybe Campbell will come back next year. His mom is still trying to get him to come back to school. Finish his last year."

"Kids are so shortsighted. Can't he see that he's going to need to finish school if he's going to get anywhere in life? What kind of a job is he going to be able to get if he doesn't even have a high school diploma? But everything has to be immediate for this generation. Instant gratification. He can't see a year or two down the line. He has to have his fun now and isn't farsighted enough to see the consequences."

"It's hard for them." Erin remembered how it had been as a high school student, trying to structure her life so that she would not end up homeless on the street. As much as she would have liked to have dropped out of school and crashed with other friends and not had to worry about money and a place to live, she had known that she had no safety net. She wasn't going to have a home. She wouldn't be able to go back to high school in the future if she didn't finish by the time she was eighteen. Unless she got a scholarship or apprenticeship, she wasn't going to get any more education. "Cam and Joshua have been through a lot lately. It's been very stressful for them. It's hard to concentrate on work or sports when there is so much traumatic stuff going on."

Coach Hadrian rolled his eyes. "Too much coddling. If these

kids were not coddled and babied so much, they would be able to withstand more of the hard knocks."

Erin stared at him. Either he had no idea of what the Cox boys had gone through—and she didn't know how he could not be aware of it—or else he didn't have any understanding and compassion for them. She turned away from him and looked for the vice principal. Facing the door, she looked down at the clock face on her phone. If the vice principal was not able to break free from whatever was occupying him, she could leave and reschedule it for a better time.

Fitzroy appeared in the doorway at that moment, catching her looking at the time. "Sorry, Miss Price. The work of a vice principal is never done," he told her jovially. "Seems like there's always something to take me away from where I have planned to be."

"I don't have a lot of time," Erin said, giving Hadrian a quick look to encourage him to be on his way.

"Thanks, Coach," Fitzroy said. "I'll catch up with you later."

Erin waited for Hadrian to go and, eventually, he nodded to Fitzroy and left the room. Fitzroy sat down at the table and smiled at Erin. "Okay, then, let's sort this out."

When Erin got out of the meeting with Fitzroy, school was about to get out. She looked around, wondering whether she would be able to spot Joshua Cox. Beaver was right, of course; she couldn't expect him to tell her all of his problems just because she wanted to help, but they had shared the experience of looking for Brianna, and maybe they had bonded a little over that and Joshua would feel like he could tell her about his problems.

She walked slowly as she left the school. If she saw him, she saw him, and she would say hello and see where the conversation led. If she didn't see him, then she wouldn't pursue it any further.

As she watched, she saw Joshua come out of the school with a couple of other boys. She tried to get close enough to get his attention and wave to him.

"Miss Erin!"

She was confused at first, thinking that Josh had called her, but he didn't call her 'miss.' She turned and looked around, and again saw Harold and one of the other boys who had been playing basketball.

"Oh, hi Harold. How are you doing?"

"What are you doing here? I thought the bake sale wasn't until Tuesday."

"No, just ironing out some details with your vice principal."

"Oh, okay."

Erin looked over at Joshua, but it was too late to catch up and get his attention. He was moving quickly away from them with his buddies.

"You know about them?" Harold asked.

Erin looked at him, feeling her brow furrow. "Do I know about them?"

"Joshua and them? You look like you know them."

"Yes, I know who Joshua is... I know his mother. Do you know him?"

Harold shrugged, his hands held wide. "He's like tenth grade. I don't *know* know him."

Erin smiled. She remembered how that was. Knowing who the older kids were, admiring them from afar, but not being part of their circle. Everyone knew who the older kids were, especially in a small town like Bald Eagles Falls.

"He seems like a nice guy," she told Harold. "It's too bad about Campbell. They've both had a lot of trouble in the last few years. I hope things will go better for them now. Maybe Campbell will come back to school. And Joshua will stay in school and be able to get back on track."

Harold scratched behind his ear. "Coach would really like to be able to get Campbell back on the sports teams. And Josh, I guess. But he wasn't ever a big star."

"Yes, I talked to Coach Hadrian, and he said he's tried to get Josh back on the team a few times, but he won't do it. And he'd love to get Campbell back, but I suspect Campbell won't be coming back to school. If he did, he would probably do some other kind of program. In the city, maybe. Continuing education or some outreach program."

"Did Coach tell you that?"

"No, just that he wished that Campbell were still here. Do you play on any of the teams? Basketball? You seemed like a pretty good player when I saw you the other day."

Harold blushed. "I'm not that good. We were just messing around."

"You didn't look too bad to me."

"Maybe when I'm older, I'll be able to get on one of his teams. But I'm still too young for the high school teams."

"I bet you won't have any trouble getting on."

He shook his head, still red-faced. His friend grinned and nudged him, some private joke between them.

Harold pushed him away, embarrassed. He looked back at Erin.

"Well… I guess I'll be seeing you around," he said.

Erin nodded. "Come by the bakery later on; we've got pumpkin muffins with chocolate chips on today."

"Oh…" Harold grinned. "Maybe I'll go by there now."

They separated, and Erin went on her way.

CHAPTER 18

There was plenty to occupy Erin's time, even on a day she was not on shift. She still had business records, accounting and advertising, and employee payrolls to be processed. And she had to look at the schedules for the coming week, both for herself and the other employees.

Aside from bakery work, she had a house to maintain and needed to keep food in the fridge and have something on the table at mealtimes. Or at least once a day.

She chopped vegetables, her hands on autopilot and her mind far away. Orange Blossom wound around her feet, waiting for something edible to fall from the sky. He seemed to be back to his normal self and she still had no idea what had made him sick.

Terry had put in a short shift and was already bouncing around the house looking for something to keep him occupied. Erin was aware of his location in the house at all times, even though she wasn't consciously trying to track him. He came into the kitchen behind her and put his hands on her waist.

Erin let him nuzzle her neck for a moment before pulling away to continue making supper.

"How was your day?" Terry asked...

"It was fine. Getting the final arrangements made on the bake sale. I hope it brings something in. I'd hate to go to all of this work for nothing."

"People will donate what they can."

"I know. I'm just worried about how much that will be."

"Melissa has been working on the toy drive. I'm glad she took it and left the rest of us to deal with police work."

"Toy drive isn't your thing?"

"I like kids, and it's a worthy cause. I'm glad we're doing it. I'm just… grateful that it isn't part of my job."

"How is she doing with it? Does she need any help?"

"As far as I can tell, she's doing just fine."

"Good."

Erin worked quietly on the vegetables.

"You seem very far away," Terry commented.

"Oh… yeah. Sorry. I keep thinking… about something one of the boys at the school said."

Terry massaged her shoulders. "What?"

"When we saw Joshua, he said, 'Do you know about them?' Not 'Do you know them?' but 'Do you know *about* them?'"

He considered. "Like they were doing something?"

Erin nodded slowly. "Yes. You know how it is when you're at school, and there's a group of kids that everyone knows about except the adults. They're drinking or cheating on tests or harassing girls. Do you know *about* them? Do you know what they're doing? What kind of people they are?"

"Hmm." Terry sat down at the table to rest. He motioned for K9 to lie down beside him and watched Erin. K9 flopped over onto his side with a thump and a groan. He almost seemed more tired on the shorter shifts than he had been when Terry had been putting in long hours. Or maybe it was boredom rather than tiredness.

Terry himself looked tired, but he was also interested in Erin's thoughts. "Do you think Joshua is involved in drugs?"

"I don't know. Beaver wouldn't say whether he was working with her as an informant, but I feel like she's keeping an eye on him, and why would she do that unless she was either worried what he was getting into or he was someone she was handling?"

"After the trouble with Campbell, maybe just because she feels guilty and wants to make sure the family doesn't suffer any more problems."

"But she would know that you can't stop kids from getting into trouble if they decide that's what they're going to do. If Joshua is going to get into trouble, he's going to get into trouble. If he's drinking or doing drugs or dealing, he's not going to stop because she warns him to."

"No, but she could threaten to arrest him. You never know, that might scare him straight."

Erin nodded slowly. "Oh, I sure hope he isn't interested in anything really bad. I really hope I'm just jumping to conclusions and there's nothing to worry about."

"You could ask your friend for more information."

"I would... but he's pretty... anxious. He's fairly new here in town, and I think he's worried about staying on the good side of the group of boys that he hangs out with. He wants to tell me things, but he's afraid that they'll think he's a rat."

"What makes you think that?"

"Just... the way he talks, the way they treat each other. I think they know something about the burglaries, or have some guesses, at least, but they don't want to come out and say it."

"You think they know about the burglaries?" Terry asked sharply. "And you're just telling me about this now?"

"Well, I don't know what it is they know about," Erin defended herself, "because they're afraid to tell me. I'm trying to find out what I can, but if they won't talk to me, I don't have anything to pass on to you."

"Except for the fact that you might know of witnesses to the burglaries and you haven't bothered to mention it. They may not be willing to say anything about it to you, but put them in separate interrogation rooms, and we would probably have everything they know in pretty short order."

Erin's stomach tightened into a knot. Harold in an interrogation room with Stayner or someone determined to scare him into talking? She couldn't do that to him. He was already nervous, not sure what to say. It would be cruel to report him to the police and let them interrogate him.

"Who is it?" Terry asked. His voice was quiet and even, carefully controlled so that he would not come across to Erin as being angry or bullying. But she knew that didn't mean anything. He still expected her to give him the names.

"I don't know if they know anything," she protested again.

"It's not your job to investigate it. It's the responsibility of the police department. You give me the information I need, and then I can talk to them to find out what they know. If they know something about the burglaries, then it's important for us to find out. That's the only way we're going to be able to figure out who this is."

He waited. Erin put the vegetables into the soup pot and put on the lid.

"Come sit down," Terry suggested.

Erin sat down and let him take her hand across the table.

"Look, you want to find out who has been targeting these families, don't you?" he asked reasonably. "These children? You said you know what it's like not to get anything special at Christmas. You want to put a stop to the burglaries so that no more children will wake up to an empty stocking Christmas morning."

"Yes," Erin agreed, "of course. We all do."

"The police department is doing everything we can to find out who it is. We're gathering as much physical evidence as we can, but there hasn't been a lot left behind. We need witnesses. People who have seen or heard something. Maybe these boys have just heard some rumors going around. It may be totally unconnected with the burglaries, or it may just be gossip. But we can't determine that until we get a chance to talk with them."

"I'll try to talk to them again," Erin suggested. "See if I can find out some more… they haven't actually said that they know anything about it. They just said that maybe it's someone from out of town. Like someone who's here to play Santa Claus during the Christmas season."

Terry nodded. "That could be important information. If they've actually heard something. If it's not just 'it can't be one of us, so it must be an outsider.'"

"I'll talk to them."

"No. You just need to give me their names, and I'll talk to them."

"Terry, I can't."

"You need to. How else are we going to solve this case?"

"I owe it to them to talk to them first."

"No, you don't. You owe it to me and the rest of the police department and Bald Eagle Falls. You know where investigating on your own has gotten you before."

Erin stiffened. She knew what he was saying, but she didn't want to hear it. "Sometimes it's led me to the truth," she pointed out. "How many times have you not believed what I had to say?"

"I believe you. That's why I want to follow up on it. But so far, all you've given me is maybe Joshua and his friends could be wrapped up in something and maybe someone who is here for temporary work."

"So look into that to start with. See where it leads."

"We will. But we need to know what the boys know. So many crimes go unsolved not because there aren't any witnesses, but because the witnesses won't come forward."

Erin shrugged and looked away from him. "I'll tell you when I can."

"Are you serious?" Terry's tone changed from the patient, encouraging one he had been using to disbelief. "You aren't going to tell me? You think you can investigate this yourself?"

"Not investigate. Just talk to these boys. See if there's anything there."

"I can go to the school and start interviewing all of the kids."

"That's a lot of people."

"Erin. Be reasonable. You know it's my job to protect Bald Eagle Falls and its residents. That's what I'm going to do."

"Yes. You're very good at your job."

Terry got to his feet abruptly. Erin shied away, even though she didn't believe he would ever do anything to hurt her. She was already anxious, and the sudden movement startled her. Terry stared at her for a minute, frustrated, then headed for the front door. K9 looked up, then jumped to his feet to follow.

"Where are you going?" Erin's voice squeaked higher.

Terry looked over his shoulder briefly. "Home. I think I need some space."

The door banged shut behind him. Erin stood and watched him walk down the sidewalk to his truck, get in with K9, and drive away.

$\mathcal{E}$rin was finding it too cold in the evening to do her tai chi outdoors, so she had switched her practice to the living room until it got warm enough to take it back outside. She worked her way through her usual routines. Despite the improvement she had made in achieving a focused and meditative state, the house felt very empty. Orange Blossom and Marshmallow watched her exercise, always a bit bemused by her actions. She knew she wasn't completely alone, but she couldn't forget Terry leaving in anger either.

They hadn't ever had a real fight before. They sometimes disagreed with each other. They got impatient and got short with each other like any couple. But she couldn't remember either of them walking out on the other before.

She had thought that he would come back. He would take a walk or a drive, blow off his steam, and come back to her, embarrassed by his actions. But he didn't. There was no sign that he was coming back.

Erin called Vic. "You want to come over for a while? I could use the company."

"Did Terry have to go out? Sure. I'll be right over."

"Okay, thanks."

Vic was in the back door a few minutes later. She joined Erin on the couch, picking up Orange Blossom and cuddling him.

"Everything okay? How's Blossom feeling?"

Erin shook her head. Her eyes filled with tears and she didn't know what to say or do, embarrassed by the show of emotion. "Oh, brother." She sniffled. "Ignore the tears. It's just... Terry."

Vic did as she was asked and made no comment on Erin's tears and didn't act like something must be dreadfully wrong. "You guys have a fight?"

"I guess. An argument. And he took off. Went home. Said he needed some space."

"Well, that's better than taking your head off or getting physical." Vic looked at Erin, waiting, too polite to ask what it was they were arguing or fighting about.

"I was talking to one of the boys at the school. Someone who might know something about the burglaries." Erin swiped at the tears that leaked down her cheeks.

"Really?"

"I don't know. Maybe. It's just a feeling. They haven't actually told me anything."

"And why was Terry upset about that? Didn't he turn up the same kids in his investigation?"

"No. Not yet, anyway. He says he'll go over to the school to talk to all of them on his own if I won't give him their names. He'll find out who it was I was talking to and interrogate them until they tell him everything they know."

Vic frowned a little. "You don't want him to know who it is?"

"Not until I know if they really know something or not. I don't want them getting dragged into the police department to tell everything they know. I wouldn't want them to be scared and their mothers all worried that they're involved in something. If they do know something, it doesn't mean they're involved, just that they heard about what's going on."

"Terry isn't going to bully them."

"You didn't hear how he was talking... and Stayner might. Or someone else. I just don't think it's fair that they get pressured because they said something to me. I don't want anyone to get in trouble."

"Okay. That's fair. So you're going to try to talk to them? Find out what you can for Terry?"

"Yes. I guess. But he's pretty ticked off about it. You know how he gets about me investigating something, even when I'm not investigating."

Vic rolled her eyes. "Well, there is historically some reason for concern. I mean… things have happened."

"You really think there's any danger in talking to some young teens to find out if they know anything?"

"No. I'm just saying he's not completely off the mark."

"I'm not telling him that someone is a witness when I'm not sure. I need to know for sure."

Vic shrugged and nodded. "That's totally up to you. If Officer Piper doesn't like it… well then, he should go home and think about it for a while. You're free to do what you think is best."

But Erin didn't find that comforting. She had made her bed, and now she had to lie in it.

And lie in it alone.

She went to bed without Terry for the first time in weeks. He had been there every night since he had been discharged from the hospital. She kept waking in the night, reaching out for him, and being disappointed to find an empty space where he should have been. They both tended to wake each other up when they had restless nights, so she had thought that she might get a better sleep with him gone, and not tossing and turning or getting up to watch TV to quiet his anxious brain. But that had not been the case. She felt like she barely slept a wink.

Vic knew better than to ask her whether she and Terry had made up. She could see when she got into Erin's car that Terry's truck was still missing. She gave Erin a sympathetic look and climbed in without asking for any additional details.

"I'll decorate the last of the Grinch cookies today," Vic offered. "Then they'll be all ready for the bake sale."

"Yeah, that will be good. We have a few more people who will be dropping off other baked goods at the school today. If anyone tries to deliver them to Auntie Clem's tell them they *have* to go to the school. I am not going to be storing gluten items at the bakery."

"Roger that."

"Roger," Erin repeated, her brain segueing to Mary Lou's husband. "Do you know whether Mary Lou is going to be able to see him for Christmas? They must allow visitors on Christmas Day."

"I would assume so," Vic said. "She hasn't said anything to me about it." Vic gave a little shrug. "But why would she?"

Erin admitted that there was no reason for Mary Lou to have to tell either of them any of her plans. She deserved some privacy.

Her mind shifted to the Cox boys.

Do you know about them?

Maybe Harold had just wondered if she knew about everything the Coxes had been through. Maybe he'd heard the stories about Roger's attempted suicide and about being committed after Joelle's death.

It could have been something as innocent as that, and she'd gone and told Terry that he thought Josh was involved in the burglaries. Now Terry was going to be looking at Joshua Cox and asking him uncomfortable questions. She felt sick at the thought.

As if the Cox family hadn't already been through enough.

CHAPTER 20

Erin's phone rang, and since it was a quiet moment, she pulled it out to see who it was. Mrs. Peach, one of her neighbors. Erin frowned. They normally didn't do anything more than nod and smile to each other if they both happened to be outside their homes at the same time. They didn't socialize. Mrs. Peach was, as far as Erin knew, a very nice old woman with thin, white hair who usually wore a flowered print dress that fell just below her knees. She had probably been one of those to call in noise violations on Erin when Orange Blossom had been yowling too loudly. But she kept an eye on things around the neighborhood, and Erin didn't hold it against her.

"Erin here."

"Is this Erin Price?"

"Yes, it is, Mrs. Peach. Is something wrong?"

"Do you know you have a broken window?"

"What? No, I had no idea! Which window is it?" She thought immediately of the little attic room where she liked to read and do her genealogical research. It seemed like attic windows would be the most likely to be broken, maybe by a bird.

"Your living room window. It's quite a large hole. You should get someone over here to cover it up until it can be fixed."

"Yes, I will. I'll pop home and have a look right now."

"Okay, then, dear. I'll be out for my morning constitutional, so I won't be here."

"Thanks for calling to let me know."

"Of course. It can't just stay like that, can it?"

Erin hung up and started to untie her apron. "Will you be able to cover for a few minutes?" she asked Vic. "It's not too busy."

"Sure. What's wrong?"

"A rock through my window or something like that. Mrs. Peach called to say that it had a hole in it. I'm going to go take a look."

"Oh, goodness. I wonder what happened?"

"I'll find out."

"I'll give Willie a call. If he's not too busy, he can have a look and see about fixing it for you."

"Okay, thanks. That would be good."

Erin pulled on a jacket and hurried out to her car. Bald Eagle Falls was such a small place, and Clementine's house was walking distance from the bakery, so Erin was there in a couple of minutes.

Even though Mrs. Peach had said it was a large hole, she wasn't prepared for it. She had been expecting something an inch or two in diameter; maybe a rock kicked up when someone was pulling out of their parking space on the street. She hadn't been expecting a gaping hole like someone had shot a cannon through it.

"What the heck happened?" Erin wondered aloud.

She hurried up the sidewalk and unlocked the door. She disarmed the burglar alarm as she stepped in the door, muttering to it that it really hadn't done her any good if it wasn't going to let her know when someone broke a window.

In the middle of the living room lay a brick. Erin stared down at it, trying to come up with a reason for it to be there other than the obvious. Who would throw a brick through her window? It had to be a mistake. Some bizarre turn of events. A rock falling out of an airplane flying overhead. Someone trying to throw a brick at an intruder. Kids playing a game.

She knew none of it was true, but she didn't know what else to think. No one would intentionally damage her house like that, would they?

She was still standing there, looking down at it, when Willie arrived. He came up behind her and stood in the doorway.

"Knock, knock?"

Erin startled at the sound of his voice. She turned and looked at him. Willie entered the house and looked into the living room. He took a sharp breath in.

"Was there a note?"

Erin looked down at it. "A note?"

"Was it a warning? Did someone tie or wrap a note around it? No?"

Erin shook her head. "No."

"Do you know… what this is about?"

"No."

"Well, if people are going to threaten you, it would at least be a courtesy to let you know why."

"Who would do something like that?"

"I don't know. Have you called Officer Piper?"

"Uh… no."

"I assume he's on duty. If he'd been here, this wouldn't have happened."

"I don't think so. They've only got him on afternoon shifts right now."

Willie frowned, looking toward the street. "Then where is he…?"

"He's at his house. Or at least, I assume he is." Erin ignored his questioning look. There was no reason Terry wouldn't be at his house. He did have a place of his own, after all. Erin hadn't been to his bachelor pad lately, but she knew the little house well and had spent a few nights there. But they had naturally fallen into the habit of Terry staying at Erin's, rather than her dropping in at his place. There were the pets, for one thing.

"Oh… where are the animals? Orange Blossom? Where are you?"

She looked behind the couch, Marshmallow's favorite hiding place, and he tilted his head slightly to look at her.

"Come on out, Marshmallow. Did that scare you?"

"Don't call him out yet," Willie warned. "Unless you want to pen him in the kitchen. You don't want him to get cut on the glass."

"Oh." Erin realized belatedly that there were shards of glass everywhere. "Oh, this is pretty bad. We'll be finding bits of glass for weeks. And if one of them eats it…"

"I don't think they're going to eat it. But we do want to get it cleaned up so that they don't walk through it."

"Come here, Marshmallow," Erin called to the rabbit once more. She liked Willie's idea of penning him in the kitchen. And Orange Blossom too, if she could get him to stay there. Maybe she'd better put him in the bathroom where she could shut the door.

Marshmallow came out to sniff at her and get his ears scratched. He kicked a little when Erin picked him up, then settled down again. Erin put him in the kitchen and put up the baby gate they had for just that purpose. She climbed back over it and went looking for the cat.

He was crouched on the bed waiting for her, his pupils wide and black, clearly spooked.

"Hey, Blossom. Did that scare you? Poor kitty." She picked him up and cuddled him. He started to purr. "Yeah, that was pretty scary, wasn't it? Were you out there when it happened?" The cat liked to sleep in the living room when she was out, finding a sunbeam to snooze in, waiting for her to get back. She looked at his paws to make sure they were okay. No blood or embedded glass. She kissed him on the head. "I know you're not going to like it, but I'm going to put you in the bathroom for a few minutes while we clean up."

He started yowling plaintively the moment she closed the door. Willie was waiting for Erin to get back.

"You're going to call the police department, right?"

Erin hesitated. What was there to report? She couldn't point to anyone or say why it had been done. They would be just as clueless as she was, unless there was a serial brick-thrower as well as a burglar.

"I don't know. Do I have to?"

He gave her a puzzled look. "I'm not sure why you wouldn't. You probably need a police file number to claim it on your insurance."

"But I could just replace it myself, too."

"Yes… you could. Is something going on with you and Terry?"

Erin shrugged. "We have a difference of opinions."

"You don't have to call him. Just call the dispatcher. If he's not on shift, they'll send someone else to deal with it."

Erin thought about Stayner and wrinkled her nose. She'd feel better if she knew it would be the sheriff or Tom taking the report. With a sigh, she pulled out her phone and, with Orange Blossom's cries still ringing in the background, reported the act of vandalism. She hung up.

"They'll send someone out right away."

"We'll wait until they see it before cleaning up. Then we'll get the glass cleaned up and cover the hole. I'll measure the window and get you a new one."

Erin tried to relax the tense muscles of her neck and shoulders. "That's really helpful, thank you. I'm not sure what I would do without you."

"You'd just ask one of your friends or the police who to call, and they'd put you in touch with someone else who could do it for you."

"Well, it's nice not to have to do that. Thanks."

"Happy to help."

It was Sheriff Wilmot who responded to the call, which calmed Erin somewhat. He was low-key and relaxed. He tugged his heavy duty belt up, looking around the living room.

"That's a nasty surprise for you," he observed. "Were you home when it happened?"

"No. A neighbor noticed and called me."

"So, no one saw it happen?"

"I assume if they had, they would have told me."

"I'll ask around just in case. See if anyone was seen behaving suspiciously."

"Carrying around a bag of bricks?" Erin asked with a laugh.

"Scoping out the house, looking nervous, or yes, carrying a brick. Or running away. You never know. It's a small community. It's not easy to get away with something like this without someone noticing something."

"Do you need anything else, or can we start cleaning up?"

"Y'all can start cleaning up, but I'd like to ask you a few questions. Do you have any idea who might do something like this?"

"I don't know. No one I can think of."

"You haven't had any threats lately, any fights or arguments with anyone?"

Erin shook her head, even though she had, of course, had an argument with Terry. That wasn't what Sheriff Wilmot was asking. Terry wasn't the kind of person who would have thrown a brick through a window, especially over something like a difference of opinions. He was a strictly law-abiding citizen and wouldn't tolerate such behavior in himself or others.

"No, nothing."

"Strange phone calls? Hang-ups or heavy breathing?"

"No."

"Ever have anything like this happen in the past?"

"No."

"So there's nothing you can think of that this could be related to? You've had some run-ins with shady characters in the past..."

"Yes... but I don't think any of them are around anymore.

Everyone has been caught, been put in jail. Or... they're not around anymore."

"Might be worthwhile to make sure that no one's been released or made bail."

"That wouldn't happen, would it? I mean, we're talking about accused murderers, drug dealers..."

"They still get out on bail regularly. Can't hurt to check."

"Yeah. I guess. You'll do that?"

Wilmot nodded. "All the ones I know. Is there anyone else that I should be aware of?"

"No."

"No one from your life before you came here? Someone who might have tracked you down?"

"You make it sound like there should be!"

The sheriff spread his hands wide. "All I know is what I've seen. And that is that you tend to... attract trouble. So it would not surprise me if you have had some... interactions with unsavory characters before you came here."

"No."

"Nobody in your past who might have been resentful and tracked you down?"

Erin shifted uncomfortably. Of course she'd had disagreements with people in the past. Run afoul of someone, been falsely accused... there had always been something. But no one who would have followed her to Bald Eagle Falls or have known that she was there.

"No."

"Okay. If you're not telling me the truth, you are the one who will suffer from it. I don't want you to be in danger because you were afraid to admit to something."

"You don't think I'm in danger, do you?" Erin clenched her fists, trying to stay calm and in control. "This is someone who wouldn't even talk to me face-to-face."

"In my experience, the type of folks who throw bricks through windows are the same ones as will use a Molotov cocktail or some other kind of violent behavior. He may not want to talk to you to your face, but people who make threats or cause property damage like this do still get violent."

Erin let that sink in. She didn't need someone else stalking her. The burglar alarm was supposed to protect her from crazies.

Terry was supposed to be there with K9 to defend her against any intruders.

They were supposed to be keeping her safe from harm.

CHAPTER 21

*E*rin stayed for long enough to get the glass cleaned up and for Willie to put cardboard over the broken window. Then he was going to order a new window and put it in for her. That would probably take a few days. Her stomach was complaining. Looking at the time on her phone, she realized that she had missed her usual early lunch hour and that Vic had been left to deal with the lunchtime rush herself.

It couldn't be helped. Erin would make it up to her another day, covering for Vic when she needed time off for something else. They were already doing that, of course...

She had a quick bite to eat, standing over the sink to catch any crumbs, then headed back to Auntie Clem's. The lunch rush was already past, and Vic didn't look too poorly for having had to weather it herself. Erin walked into the kitchen and grabbed her apron, apologizing to Vic.

"Sorry to be so long, we had to call the police, and deal with making a report, and we just got everything swept up and covered. I didn't mean to take so long."

"It's fine. I did all right."

"You did take a lunch break, right?"

"I did. So what's the scoop? Was it a bird? A rock?"

Erin looked blankly at her.

"What broke your window?" Vic asked.

"Oh. Sorry, I was thinking about lunch! No birds or rocks for lunch."

Erin told her as much as she could about the brick, which wasn't very much other than that it had been thrown through the window. There wasn't anything about the brick itself that would help the police figure out who had thrown it.

It was almost closing time when Terry came by. That was not unusual; he liked to stop by at the end of the day to see how she was, to help tidy up and consume stray cookies that had not sold during the day. It was a relaxed end-of-day ritual that they all enjoyed, including K9, who would lie down nibbling a gluten-free doggie biscuit.

But that ritual had ceased when Terry had been injured and gone off of active duty. And although he was back to acting as a policeman part-time, he hadn't started coming by again.

So for an instant, Erin's heart rose when she saw him coming up to the door. Things were finally getting back to normal. He was going to start coming by at the end of the day again, and she would get to spend some quiet time with him just tidying up and getting ready for the next day.

But when she saw his face, she knew that he wasn't there to help her to clean up and get ready for the next morning. She had become accustomed to seeing the fatigue and worry on his face more often than the dimple that appeared when he was really smiling about something. But that didn't compare to the thunder-cloud that was over him as he stepped into the bakery.

He didn't slam the door open or send the bells jingling wildly. If anything, he opened it more slowly and quietly than he usually did. But that didn't stop the cold chill that raced through Erin.

She looked quickly over at Vic, who raised a questioning eyebrow, also wondering what was going on.

"Why didn't you call me?" Terry demanded without preamble.

"Call you?"

"About the brick through your window. Why didn't you call me and let me know what had happened?"

Erin hesitated, not sure she was willing to answer. Not sure if there was an answer that would soothe him, or if any response would be wrong. "I just called the dispatcher. I didn't think you would be on duty."

"I wasn't. But what does that have to do with it? I would still think that I would be your first phone call when you have something to be concerned about. Especially something like this, where you called the police to make a report."

Erin was silent. It didn't feel right to tell him that she normally would have called him first. That had been her first instinct. But that she hadn't because they had argued and he had left, and she didn't feel right about being the one to call him. She was still waiting for him to apologize for his anger and for leaving her alone.

She poured a finished muffin batter into a bowl to soak and set it to the side. She rinsed out the mixing bowl and started the next batch. She kept her eyes down, waiting for him to finish talking and either leave or lend a hand and go home with her.

"Erin, you should have called. Did you think I wouldn't come?"

He waited. Erin kept working. She was glad to have something to keep her hands and brain busy. She didn't want to think about that. How horrible it would be to call him and not have him come running. Is that why she had been so hesitant?

"I'm sorry," he said softly, but with an urgency behind his words. "I shouldn't have pushed you when you said that you weren't going to tell me the names of your witnesses. I should have just waited until you'd had a chance to think about it and were ready. And I shouldn't have just walked out on you."

"You said you needed space. You're allowed to go home whenever you want to. You're not obligated to stay with me. It's your choice."

"I know that. That isn't what I meant. I'm not dumping you; I just needed to think."

Erin nodded.

"So are we okay?" Terry asked.

"Sure," she said curtly.

Terry looked at Erin, then glanced over at Vic. It was awkward to be having the discussion in front of her, but he had chosen the time and the place. He had known that Vic had work to do there and couldn't just politely excuse herself.

"So… tell me about the happenings at your house today." His voice was casual, but his expression was not. He sat down on one of the stools she kept in the kitchen for when she needed to be off her feet. His eyes were intense and focused. He was in investigation mode.

"Not much to tell," Erin said with a shrug. "I imagine you got it all from Sheriff Wilmot's report. There wasn't much to say."

"An unknown person threw a brick through your window."

"Yes."

"No witnesses?"

"None that I know of. He was going to canvass, ask around."

"But the house wasn't broken into?"

"No."

"Nothing stolen."

"No. It wasn't a burglary. Just a brick through the window."

"But no note warning you to stay away from a certain place or event. No hint of what this might be about."

"No."

"It has to be related to the burglaries."

"Really? Do you think so?" Erin considered, and shook her head. "I don't see the connection. Why do you think that?"

"What is the one thing you have been asking questions about and poking your nose into that people might not like? The burglaries. You're the one who knows that Joshua might be involved. Who got a tip or two from unnamed witnesses. You've rubbed someone the wrong way."

"I haven't been asking questions. All I've been doing when I talk to anyone at the school is getting the bake sale preparations done. If someone is offended by me asking if they'll make some cookies or tarts for the bake sale, then yeah, maybe one of them threw a brick through my window. But most of the ladies I have talked to haven't seemed to be the brick-throwing type."

"If you haven't been asking any questions, then how did you find out that Joshua could be involved? And how do you know that someone might know something that we don't? People don't just walk up to you and tell you things like that."

"No, that's why I need to see if I can get some more information from him. But I didn't *do* anything; I just talked to them casually. A couple of times. He said just enough to make me wonder if he knows anything. But he might not. He might think he does, or he might just be teasing me, trying to show off to his friends."

"Let the sheriff and I work that out. I don't understand what your objection is to this."

"You're not going to talk me into it," Erin said forcefully.

Terry leaned back from her, looking startled.

"You say you're sorry for pushing me, and then you start pushing again," Erin pointed out. "Just stop it."

"You need to come in and at least tell the sheriff about the witness. Even if you don't want to talk to me about it for some reason, he needs to know that there is a witness."

"No."

"Erin. You need to turn over the names of anyone who might be a witness. You can be compelled to tell what you know."

"You can't compel me. Are you really going to drag me before a judge? You can't make me go in and make a statement."

He searched for something to say to change her mind, but Erin just shook her head. She put the last bowl in the sink and ran hot water. Vic gathered up any other utensils or dishes that needed to be washed and added them to the sink.

They worked together in silence, with Terry hovering over them trying to think of a way to force her to tell what she knew. Erin washed up and put everything away.

"Are you coming to the house?"

"Maybe I'd better not."

Erin gave one nod. "Fine. I'll see you later, then."

After he was gone, Vic gave Erin a wide-eyed look. "Whoa. You're really not backing down on this, are you? I've never seen the two of you so at odds with each other, not even at that first case."

"He has some issues. He's still recovering from a head injury, and he's not feeling that great. I think... if he was feeling his normal self, it wouldn't be an issue. So I'll wait... until he's back to himself again."

"But what if he doesn't go back to the way he was? It is possible for people to change, especially after a head injury. What if this is the new normal?"

Erin took a deep breath and let it out again. "Then I'd better either get used to it or move on."

She wasn't going to stay in a relationship where her partner thought he could push her around.

CHAPTER 22

Knowing that Terry wasn't likely to be returning to her house until Erin gave him the name of her potential witness, Erin decided she'd better push forward and find out more. She'd been hesitant to pursue it in the pre-Christmas season. Everyone was in such a rush and had so much stress already that she didn't want to push them. Especially when so many families were dealing with the burglaries, wondering how they were going to be able to have Christmas. Erin didn't think that Harold's family was one of the ones that had been targeted, but she wasn't sure.

Either way, if Harold knew something about who had been breaking into people's houses and stealing their presents, Erin had to find out what it was and relay it to the police department. She didn't want to be still fighting with Terry when Christmas Day came around. She'd had enough miserable Christmases in the past.

She looked up Harold's address. She was surprised to see that he lived at one of the farms outside the city. She had thought that, being new, he would be right inside town. She had assumed that they were city people. After studying the map to make sure she knew the way to his house, she drove over, hoping that she would not arrive during their supper hour.

She wanted to get there early enough that his parents wouldn't find it creepy that she was calling on their son. She wasn't sure how she was going to explain that she thought their son might know something about the burglaries if the door were answered by one of the parents. Did she just say, "is Harold available?" or did she explain herself in detail?

With any luck, they wouldn't even be home, but Harold would. She wasn't sure where she was going to find him if he wasn't at home. He might be at the school again, playing a pickup basketball game. Or maybe at a friend's house.

But she was in luck. Harold answered the door himself and his parents were not in evidence.

"Miss Erin?" He stepped back from the door to allow her to enter. "What are you doing here?"

She let him close the door and seat her in the living room before trying to explain.

"I'm glad I found you at home, Harold. I was worried that you might be out with friends and I really wanted to talk to you."

"Well, you weren't actually so lucky. I don't have a lot of friends."

"You were playing basketball the other day, and with another friend yesterday."

"Yeah, I hang out a little with them. But we're not really... friends."

"Oh. Okay. Anyway, that's not the point. What I mean is... I wanted to know... you seem like you know about the burglaries. And I wanted to find out what you do know."

His eyes slid to the side. Erin tried to make him more comfortable.

"I know this is kind of coming out of nowhere... but you said a couple of things and I'd like to know. Do you know who has been stealing people's presents?"

Harold scratched his ear. "No."

"You don't have any idea?"

He tapped his toes and looked around some more, refusing to meet her eyes. "I dunno."

"Harold… whoever it is has messed things up for a lot of families. If you think you know something, you should share it with me. Or with the police."

"I know that, but… I don't really know anything."

"I think you do. Or maybe one of the other boys has been bragging and you were repeating what they said. It doesn't matter how you know…"

"I don't really know anything." He shook his head more vigorously. "Sometimes…" A shrug with one shoulder. "Sometimes, you overhear something. Or like you said, someone is talking about it, but you don't know if it's true or not, you just know that it's interesting. That people are repeating it."

"And you'd like a little attention too, so you start to collect some of these things…"

"I don't want to get anyone in trouble. And I don't want to get in trouble. It isn't anything."

"You asked me if I knew about Joshua. Is Joshua Cox involved?"

"No." Harold shook his head. "Joshua is a good guy. He wouldn't do something like that."

"So who would? Do you know someone who has been involved?"

"No. I don't, Miss Erin, honest."

"You said maybe it was someone new in town, maybe someone here doing seasonal work like one of the Santas. Is that who it is?"

"I don't know. Maybe. I don't really know."

Erin let that sit for a few moments. It didn't sound right. It didn't sound believable.

"How does the burglar know which houses to hit?"

Harold's face started to turn red.

"Harold?"

"I don't know anything."

"Is it someone at the school?"

"I don't know." A pause. A defeated shrug of his shoulders. "Probably."

"It's probably someone from school, or you know for sure it is someone from school?"

"I don't know for sure." But he looked away from her again. His forehead was sweating, and he wiped it with the back of his hand.

"But it is probably someone from school."

Harold nodded.

"Someone you know?"

"I don't know many people. I'm still pretty new here."

"What else can you tell me about them?"

"Don't say 'them.' Say 'him.'"

Erin had meant 'them' as a generic singular pronoun, but Harold had clearly been spooked by it. She cocked her head. "Does that mean it is more than one person? It's a group?"

"I never said that."

"No. But I think it could be. That's what Beaver said too. She thought it was probably more than one person, because of the different times of the day. And she probably knows other facts she couldn't share with me too. I'm not exactly part of the investigation. The police always hold things back from the general public."

"I never said it was anyone. I don't know who is involved."

"But maybe you have heard rumors… that it is a group of kids from school?"

"It could be anyone," Harold argued. His voice climbed a little higher. "I don't know who's doing it. I'm not involved, and I never would be. Everyone knows that. They'd never ask me."

"So this business about maybe it being one of the Santas, that was just misdirection? Trying to throw people off the trail?"

"I don't know. It could be."

"But if it was one of the Santas, he wouldn't be someone going to your school."

Harold looked down at the floor.

"You can tell me more," Erin encouraged. "You look like you need to get it off your chest. How long have you been holding on to this?"

Her sympathy affected him. His eyes became shiny with tears. "Miss Erin, you know I wouldn't be involved in anything like this."

"I know that, Harold. I wouldn't be here if I thought you were. It wouldn't be very smart of me to walk right into the home of someone I thought was involved in the burglaries, would it?"

"No," Harold agreed, giving a little laugh and wiping surreptitiously at his eyes. "It wouldn't."

"I don't think you're involved or have done anything wrong. But you need to tell someone what you know. We want to catch these guys. Everybody who knows something needs to come forward with the information they have so that the police can put them away. Then everyone can breathe a sigh of relief and be able to have their Christmases. A happy Christmas, instead of worrying about their gifts being stolen."

"I don't know anything, though, not really."

"But the little bits that you do know, put together with what others know, could lead to a break in the case."

He stared down at his feet. "Maybe."

"Will you think about it? I don't want to force you, but you know it's the right thing to do."

He shrugged. Erin decided to leave it at that.

For the present.

CHAPTER 23

*D*riving back to town, Erin pondered over what to do. She had asked Harold to think about going to the police, but she was worried he wouldn't make the right decision. He was too nervous about whatever it was he knew. If he decided not to go to the police, what was she to do? Would she go to Terry, forcing Harold to talk to them? She wanted the burglaries to be solved, for everyone to be able to relax and have a good Christmas without worrying about their houses being broken into. With any luck in the fundraising efforts, they would be able to ensure that all those who had been victims of the burglar had presents for their children. If the burglar were behind bars, no one would have to live in fear that they would be the next victim.

Erin was startled out of her reverie by a heavy thud. She tightened her grip on the steering wheel instantly, trying to keep control of the car and assess what had happened.

Her first thought was that something had gone wrong internally. Terry and Vic kept telling her that she needed to replace her car before it broke down at the most inopportune time. She had said she wouldn't use it out of town, and then she had.

Her eyes swept the dashboard for any lights, then looked in the rearview mirror and realized that the truck right on her tail had bumped her and was still only inches from her. Was he having mechanical problems, or had she been driving below the speed limit and he had gotten frustrated and bumped her intentionally?

The road was only a single lane, but there was a wide shoulder, so Erin pulled carefully to the right, giving him enough room to pull past her.

As he pulled forward to pass her, he clipped the corner of her bumper and the car slewed, coming dangerously close to rolling into the ditch. Erin held to the wheel for dear life, swearing at him in her head.

What did he think he was doing?

Erin inched the car left again, trying to avoid the ditch. But the truck was still right behind her, refusing to pass and riding her bumper. What was he was doing?

Erin pressed the gas pedal down gently, increasing her acceleration, trying to pull a safer distance ahead of the menacing vehicle.

Was he trying to kill her? She still couldn't let go of the idea that maybe he was having mechanical problems. Maybe his brakes were not working, or he had some foreign object wedged under the pedal. Or maybe he was having a heart attack or seizure. He could be confused, pressing the accelerator instead of the brake.

But as she sped up, he sped up too, staying right with her and bumping her again. Erin looked over at her purse, trying to figure out if she could get her phone out without losing control of the car.

Speeding up hadn't solved the problem. Now she was going faster, more likely to lose control of the car on a curve or if he hit her again.

She moved her foot back over to the brake and pressed it slowly down, hoping that he would back off as he saw she was slowing. She could feel the truck pressing against the bumper as she braked. The smell of burning rubber filled the air as she was braking, but the truck was shoving her forward.

Then the truck fell back, separating from her car and putting some space between them. Erin let out a pent-up breath, relieved. She continued to slow, looking for a good place to pull over. She would pull off of the highway completely, let him pass her, and call Terry for help. He'd make sure she got home without any further problems.

She heard the rush of a revving engine, and then the blow to the back left corner of her bumper. The back of the car lifted slightly from the road. Erin was helpless to stop the spin of the vehicle and correct its heading. She braced as the car headed through the shoulder and nose-first into the ditch. Even as she tried to hold herself stiff and still, she remembered that the reason so many drunks survived accidents they had caused while their victims in the other vehicle did not was because they stayed relaxed on impact. But she was scared to death, and there was no way she could relax her body as the car plunged into the ditch, cartwheeling once and coming down on its roof, then rolling over and over until it came to a shuddering stop, wheels down, facing the direction she had come from.

*E*rin didn't know how much time passed as she sat there in the car. She waited for the driver of the other vehicle to get out and check on her, but he didn't. Maybe he had gone off of the road or been injured as well. Or maybe he had gone on ahead to get help.

She closed her eyes and sat there, waiting, for what seemed to be a long time. A few times, she opened her eyes and looked around, but she didn't feel any compelling reason to move or get out of the car. She couldn't see her purse and wasn't sure where it had bounced to while the car was doing its acrobatics down the embankment.

The water in the ditch wasn't deep. That was a good thing. Erin wasn't sure what she would have done if water had started creeping up her ankles. Or worse.

Her phone started to ring. She looked around for it. It was hard to move. The phone had rung quite a number of times before she was able to find it in the back seat. She managed to unbuckle her seatbelt and leaned around the seat to retrieve the phone. She tapped the screen to answer it and put it to her ear.

"Hello?"

"Erin? Where are you? I drove by your house, and your car

wasn't there. I just wanted to make sure you are okay." It was Terry's voice.

Erin blinked, considering. "What time is it?"

"Did I wake you up? Is the car in the shop?"

"No, not yet. Will you call them?"

"You want me to call the mechanic?" Terry's voice was uncertain. "What's wrong with it? Did you get stranded?"

"I guess so," Erin admitted, looking around.

"Where? Are you somewhere safe?"

"I'm not sure where I am. There… isn't anyone else here…"

Terry's voice took on greater urgency. "Erin. *Where are you?*"

"I'm just waiting here. I thought he would get someone to help."

"Who?"

"The other driver. I thought he was getting someone."

"The other driver. Were you in an accident?"

"Yes."

He swore under his breath, but loudly enough that she could hear him. "Do you know where you are? Did you go to the city?"

"No. To see Harold."

"Who is Harold?"

"He's a customer. Comes to the bakery."

"Where does Harold live?"

"Out on a farm. After the Bushman's turnoff."

"What's his family name?"

"Melville. They're new here."

"Melville. Okay, I'm going to come out and find you. Are you in your car?"

"Yes."

"Are you on the highway?"

"Well… sort of…" Erin wasn't sure how to answer.

"What do you mean, sort of?" Terry asked, frustration clear in his voice.

"I mean… I was. But I went off the highway."

"You turned off onto another road?"

"No, I went into the ditch."

"Good grief. Are you hurt?"

This hadn't occurred to Erin before. She looked down at herself. "I don't know. I don't think so. I don't see any blood."

"I'm on my way. Do you want to stay on the phone with me?"

"Sure," Erin agreed. She leaned back, trying to relax. She closed her eyes and rested with the phone still to her ear. She could hear Terry moving around, calling to K9, the sound of his doors slamming. The low rumble of his truck's engine.

"I'm coming. Just hang in there," Terry encouraged.

"I'm okay."

"That's good. Keep talking to me, so I know you haven't passed out. What happened? You said there was another car."

"Yeah. A truck. Like yours."

"How was it like mine? A pickup? What color?"

"Yeah, big pickup like yours. I don't know… dark… maybe black."

"Could you see the driver? Did he talk to you? You said you thought he was going to go get help."

"No… he didn't stop. I just thought he must have gone to get help because he didn't stay here."

"What happened? How did the accident occur?"

"He hit me from behind. Forced me into the ditch."

"Was he following too close? Going too fast?"

"Yeah."

"And then he just takes off after the accident. Coward. I'll have him up on hit and run, you can trust me on that one."

"How will you know?"

"Because he won't be able to get it fixed without the police department being notified. We will get him."

"Okay." Erin was feeling very tired. She didn't know how long it would take Terry to find her and thought she might take a nap while she was waiting. It was night, and she wasn't sure if he'd be able to find her in the darkness. She might have to wait until morning when the sun rose and he could see the car from the highway.

"Erin!"

"Hmm?" Erin tried to rouse herself. "I'm tired, Terry."

"I know you are. But you need to wait until I get there to evaluate you. Keep talking to me so that I know you're okay."

Erin took a deep breath. She was just so tired. "Okay. I'll try."

"Were you going to see the Melville boy or were you on your way back?"

"Back."

"And can you tell me whether you went into the ditch on the right side or the left?"

It took Erin a moment to orient herself and work out which side was right and which was left.

"Off the right."

"That's the passenger side. Is that right? You went into the ditch on the passenger side?"

"Yes."

"Good. I don't know how far out you are. I'm working my way along the shoulder."

"It's dark."

"I know it is," he agreed.

"You won't be able to see me. Maybe you should just come back in the morning."

"I am not waiting until morning to look for you. I'll find you tonight so that I know you're safe and being taken care of."

"Okay."

"I'll find you. I promise."

Erin waited. She couldn't think of anything to say, so she hummed to herself. It was getting harder and harder to stay awake, but she tried to do as he had told her.

A light flashed by the window. Erin thought it must be the first car that had driven down the highway since she had crashed there. It flitted past her and was gone.

"I saw a light," she told Terry.

"You did?" The light stopped moving away from her, then slowly started to move toward her again. "Can you see that?"

"Yes."

"Tell me when it's closest to you."

Erin watched the light approaching, trying to time her answer for when it was exactly beside her. "Now!"

She was a little late. It had overshot slightly, but it stopped. She heard a car door slam.

"I'm here, Erin. I'm going to come down to you."

"It's kind of steep. Be careful."

In a few moments, she could see another light bobbing toward her. There were a few missteps when the light moved to one side or the other, but it kept coming until it was right up beside her. Terry tried the door. No luck. He switched the powerful flashlight to his other hand. "Is the door locked?"

Erin felt blindly for the switch. She knew where it was, but she couldn't quite find it. Then her fingers finally encountered it. She switched first one direction, then the other, not sure which was which. Usually, the car unlocked when she parked it and she locked it with her key fob after getting out.

Terry tried the handle again and this time it clicked as the catch opened. He pulled on the door, and it creaked and protested until he finally got it unstuck and pulled it open.

"Erin."

His fingers went first to her throat, finding her pulse.

"How are you feeling? Can you tell me if it hurts anywhere?"

"I don't know. Not really. I'm getting stiff. It's cold."

"The temperature is dropping and I don't know how long you've been here. The car is pretty beaten up—did it roll?"

"Yes."

"I'm going to get a rescue team out here. I don't want to move you, in case your neck or back are injured."

"I don't think they are."

"If you damaged your spinal cord, you might not feel any

pain, even though you were hurt. You might think you were okay."

"But I can move." Erin moved her arms creakily to show him. "The phone was in the back," she motioned to the footwell where she had found it. "I got that okay."

"That's good. But I want to be one hundred percent sure. If the car rolled… you could have a lot of damage you don't know about. You're in shock. It's cold; I don't want to assume you're not hurt and do more damage."

"I want to go home."

"I know. It's just going to be a little longer."

"Can I go to sleep now?"

"I'm going to get some blankets, and then I'll sit with you while we wait for the paramedics. I can wake you up and check on you now and then."

"Okay."

She closed her eyes when he walked away and the light disappeared again, up and over the embankment. He startled her when he got back, reaching in to tuck blankets around her. Erin was grateful for his kindness, tears welling up unexpectedly in her eyes.

"I'm sorry," she apologized. "I don't know why I'm crying."

"It's all right. You're allowed to cry. You've been through something pretty traumatic. Help is on its way. We'll get you out of here soon."

Erin wiped at the tears running down her cheeks. "I don't like crying."

He leaned in, putting one hand against her cheek and kissing the other. "It's okay. You don't need to be embarrassed about crying. I know how strong you are."

CHAPTER 25

*E*rin awoke again to the sound of voices. Not just Terry's voice this time, but several others as well. There were more lights; some stationary lights pointed at the car and some flashlights in hand. Erin rubbed her eyes, but she got a chill and put her hands under the blanket again.

"Can I go home now?"

"You need to let the paramedics check you out. They'll see that you're removed from the car safely and get the treatment you need."

"Ma'am?" One of the paramedics was in front of her. "Can you tell me your name?"

"Erin Price."

"How about the date?"

Erin did her best to dredge it up from her memory but wasn't sure she got it right.

"And how about the President of the United States?"

She wasn't likely to get that one wrong.

"Can you tell me what happened to you, ma'am? How did you get here?"

Erin stifled a yawn and shifted around. "Can I just go home? I'm exhausted. I need to get home and get some sleep."

"We need to check your mental state as part of our examination." He took her pulse. "How did you get here?"

"In my car."

"Yes, ma'am," he agreed with a chuckle. "And how did that happen? You drove down here?"

"Got hit from behind. Rolled down into the ditch."

"Can you tell me if you are in any pain?"

"No. I just want to get out of here."

"I understand that. I want you to follow my finger with your eyes. Don't move your head."

Erin followed his instructions.

"And can you squeeze my fingers tight with both hands?"

Erin squeezed. She closed her eyes, tiring of the paramedic's requirements.

"Stay with me, ma'am. How long have you been here?"

"I don't know. Early evening. It wasn't dark yet."

"You didn't call for help?"

Erin was at a loss to explain it. "I don't know why not," she said finally. "I just didn't think of it."

"We're going to get you out of here now, okay?"

"Okay." Erin leaned forward, ready to get out of the car. But the paramedics had other ideas. She waited again while they discussed the best way to transport her. Eventually, they put a collar on her and two of them removed her and laid her on a backboard. Erin rolled her eyes.

"We don't need to do this. I didn't hurt my neck or back."

"We'll just take all reasonable precautions. Once the hospital has cleared you, they'll remove the collar and get you in a regular bed."

"I don't want to go to the hospital. I want to go home."

"You will. But first, you're going to the hospital to get checked out."

Erin knew that even in the best-case scenario, one where they said she was just fine and could be released from the hospital, it would still be hours before she got home.

"Terry?"

"I'm here, Erin. What is it?"

"Can you call Vic? I'm going to need someone to take my shift at the bakery."

"Yes, I'll let her know," he agreed with a chuckle. "Doesn't sound like there's anything wrong with your head."

At the hospital, Erin closed her eyes, finally able to go to sleep. But every few minutes, it seemed like someone new needed to ask her the same questions and to poke and prod her. She felt ridiculous. She was perfectly fine, and everyone was acting like she should be a wreck. There were blood samples taken, her vital signs were continuously monitored and, eventually, she was taken to x-ray so that they could have a look at her spine and make sure there was no damage. It didn't matter how many times Erin said she was okay; they had to verify it for themselves.

She was separated from Terry much of the time. At some point, he had purchased a crossword puzzle book, which he worked his way through while waiting for her.

Finally, a doctor appeared at her bedside who confirmed that she didn't have a broken back or neck and it was safe to remove her collar and the backboard. Erin tipped and turned her neck and rolled her shoulders, trying to work out the stiffness from having them kept in the same position for so long.

"So, can I go home?" she asked the doctor impatiently.

He looked over her chart, reluctant to tell her yes. But eventually, he shrugged. "It wouldn't hurt to keep you under observation for a while, but if you're intent on going home… then yes. You can be released. You might be stiff for a few days but, considering the accident you were in, I am amazed that you don't have any major injuries. You must have a guardian angel."

Erin laughed. A guardian angel for an atheist?

"Do you have a way to get home?" the doctor inquired, ignoring her mirth.

"That would be me," Terry said from behind him.

The doctor turned and nodded at Terry. "Good. I don't want her overexerting herself. She should take it easy for a few days."

Terry raised his eyebrows. "Good luck with that. I'm not sure she knows how to relax."

"You need to," the doctor said earnestly, speaking to Erin. "While we can't point to any visible injuries, you will still have suffered some soft tissue damage and have had quite a shock to your system. I want you to be careful."

"I'll be careful. But I have the bake sale to look after, and we have a lot of work to do at the bakery to make sure everyone is ready for Christmas, and—"

"Don't do too much. Have someone give you a hand. Delegate some of these jobs. What if you had been killed in this accident, who would have taken over then?"

Erin looked at him, startled. She thought about it. If things had gone differently, she could very well have had the opposite outcome. And then who would have taken over? Vic and Charley would have had to take charge. There were enough other employees that they could keep things running while they sorted out the long-term impact of Erin's death. And then what? Would they keep Auntie Clem's open, or would they shut it like they had closed The Bake Shoppe after Angela Plaint's death? She hated to think of anyone closing Auntie Clem's. They had worked so hard to keep it running, despite everything that had happened.

"I'll… I'll try to get some help," she agreed.

"Good. Take the opportunity to enjoy the Christmas season. A lot of people work too hard to enjoy it. Don't be one of them."

"I'm not really big on Christmas."

He shook his head at this answer. "You deserve some time off. Take this as a sign that you need to."

Erin slid her feet off of the bed and got to her feet, holding on to the bed for a moment to make sure she was steady. "I just had a vacation," she grumbled.

"If you want to call being attacked while solving international crimes a vacation," Terry said wryly.

The doctor's eyes widened. "That doesn't sound relaxing," he agreed. "Exactly what is it you do? Are you an FBI agent?"

"No. Just a baker," Erin told him over her shoulder, as she and Terry walked away.

CHAPTER 26

*E*rin slept quite late the next day. She wasn't usually able to sleep much past her usual rising time, but her body obviously knew that she needed it. When she awoke, she found that, as the doctor had warned, she was pretty sore. Not bruised, but like she'd had a tough workout a day or two before.

The bedroom door opened, and Terry peeked in at her.

"Hey, you're awake."

"Yeah." Erin stretched painfully and massaged her muscles and joints. "What time is it?"

"What time it is doesn't matter. The question is whether you've had enough sleep. Everything is taken care of; you don't need to worry about work."

"I'm not. Just wondering how late it is."

Terry opened the door the rest of the way to enter the room. He sat down on the side of the bed.

"It's ten. But you can spend all day in bed if you need to."

"I know."

"How are you feeling?"

Erin stopped massaging her shoulders and allowed him to take over, rubbing them gently.

"Just sore. And tired. Nothing major."

"Good. You'll need to be careful for a while, make sure your body has a chance to recover." He shook his head. "After seeing that car in the daylight… I can't believe that you got through it without any injuries. It's impossible."

"Is it really bad?"

"It's time for you to get a new car. Of course, I have been telling you that for a while now."

"I know… but if I had, then the new car would be wrecked, and I'd have to get *another* one."

Terry chuckled. "That's true. I guess your timing is perfect. Just don't get into any more accidents after you replace it."

Erin nodded her agreement.

"Do you want anything to eat?"

When Erin moved to get up, Terry held up his hands to stop her. "I will bring you breakfast in bed. Whatever you order."

Erin knew she'd better not order anything too elaborate. Terry was an excellent policeman, but his culinary skills were not stellar.

"Well… I'm not sure how much I am up to yet. I don't usually have much to eat when I first wake up. Maybe… tea and toast?"

"Your wish is my command."

He gave a little bow and left the room to prepare her breakfast. Erin settled back into her pillow and closed her eyes while she waited.

She hadn't meant to fall back asleep, but she awoke drowsily to Terry putting the breakfast down on the side table.

"Sorry," he apologized. "Do you want this? I can make more later if you want to go back to sleep."

"No, it's okay. I didn't mean to go back to sleep. I'll eat it now."

He transferred the breakfast tray to Erin's lap as she struggled to sit up the rest of the way. He helped with her pillows and then hovered, waiting to see if there was anything else she needed.

"This is good. Relax."

"Are you sure? Do you want something else on the toast? Some of the Jam Lady jam or some honey?"

"No. I don't think I'm up for that yet. This is fine."

He stood there for another moment, then sat on the edge of the bed again. A bit farther away this time so that she had the room to enjoy her meal.

"So… I know sometimes it can be hard to remember something traumatic like a car accident," Terry offered. "A lot of people can't remember how they got into a wreck. Sometimes it comes back to them again later, and sometimes it never does."

"I remember it. Most of it, anyway, I think."

"You said it was a truck like mine. What do you remember about it?"

Erin pondered while she nibbled a triangle of toast. "It was a big pickup, like yours, with the extended cab. I don't remember much else about it. It was dark, I think. Maybe black."

"Could you see anything inside? Hanging from the mirror? A load in the bed?"

"No… I don't remember. I couldn't take more than a couple of quick glances. I was trying to keep control of the car and to figure out what he was doing. I couldn't understand… why he was right on my tail. I wasn't going that slow."

"Why do you think he was?"

Erin bit her lip. She sipped her tea, not wanting to answer right away. She didn't want to make an official statement. But she supposed it would be required. If it wasn't one thing, it was another.

"I really don't know. At the time, I didn't have time to think about it. I was just trying to get out of his way. I thought maybe he was having mechanical problems with the truck. The brakes weren't working. Something like that."

"And now? What do you think now that you've had time to think about it and consider the possibilities?"

"I guess… that it must have been intentional. I tried to get to the shoulder, out of his way. He didn't pass me, even when he had plenty of room and no traffic coming the other way. When I tried to slow down, he hit me, was pushing me forward. Then I sped up and he dropped back, and I thought that it had worked."

He nodded and waited for the rest of the story.

"But I guess he dropped back to get some momentum. He put on the gas, and then hit me again, hard. Forced me off the road." Erin shook her head. "It was so scary. I knew that I should relax my body to avoid getting injured, but I was holding tight for all I was worth."

"Good thing you were wearing a seatbelt. That's the kind of accident where people get thrown from the car and crushed."

"It was crazy. When he hit me, it cartwheeled." Erin demonstrated the movement with her toast. "Then rolled over going down into the ditch. Everything was flying all over the place inside. I didn't know which way was up. Glad it landed right side up."

"I'm just glad that I could open the door and we didn't need the Jaws of Life. I was relieved to be able to touch you and reassure both of us that you were okay."

"Yeah."

"So… it sounds like it was deliberate. This guy's goal was to run you off the road. It wasn't an accident or a mechanical issue."

Erin's stomach tightened in a knot. "Where's Orange Blossom? I thought he'd be in here with me."

Terry studied her. "You were asleep. He was looking for more attention. I fed him and played with him. He's napping in the sunshine right now."

"Oh, good. He's okay?"

"Who do you think would want to hurt you?" Terry persisted. "This wasn't just to scare you. Someone intended to do you harm."

"I don't want to think about it."

"That's not going to help us. We need to find this guy. Next time, you might not be so lucky."

"I don't think I'm going to feel like driving on the highway again any time soon. Besides, I don't have a car."

"But you don't know how he'll come after you the next time.

It won't necessarily be a car accident. Someone threw a brick through your window. They know where you live. Next time, they could attack you in person."

Erin felt nauseated. She pushed the toast away and sipped the tea, hoping it would help to settle her stomach.

"You think this is because of the burglaries."

Terry nodded slowly. He took her hand and held it between his two hands, warm and strong, soothing. "Somebody doesn't like you asking questions. They are worried you are going to find out the truth and expose them."

Erin licked her lips, her mouth dry. *Them.* There were more of them, not just one person.

"Do you think it is a group acting together?" she asked Terry. "Like a gang?"

"We think it is probably a group. They get in and out of houses pretty quickly. Strike at different times of the day or night. We haven't been able to pin down any one person who had the opportunity for every one of the burglaries, they all have alibis for one or two of them."

"Yeah."

"You think so too?"

Erin nodded.

"Maybe not a gang like you are thinking of," Terry went on. "Not like a motorcycle gang or a street gang. But a group of people organized and working in concert. It lets them get away with things that they wouldn't be able to otherwise. But it is also more dangerous for them, because the more people who know, the bigger the chances are there will be a leak."

"I just can't figure it out."

"You don't need to. That's up to me. Up to the police department."

Erin let out her breath in a long sigh. Tears prickled her eyes again. "Harold Melville is one of the boys who I thought might know something."

"I figured as much."

But Terry was there with her, not at the police department offices interrogating him.

"I didn't want him to be treated like a suspect. To be bullied and scared into talking. He's my friend. He's just a kid."

"We know our jobs, Erin. He'll be okay. But we need to find out what he knows."

"He doesn't really know much. Just rumors. Just things going around the school. Probably everyone else knows the same things."

"Then it's time that some of them open up."

Erin covered her eyes, wishing that she were asleep again, not thinking about Harold and how he was going to feel about her turning him in to the police. So much for the happy, friendly kid who stopped by the bakery for a muffin or granola bar after school.

"Think about the damage being done by the burglaries," Terry said quietly. "Not just the financial losses, but how they make the victims feel. Vulnerable. Violated. Despair over the loss of everything they had planned for Christmas, maybe saving all year for it. And one day, they're going to make a mistake and hit a place where the owners are home. And then we could have more than just a burglary to deal with. You already know that they don't have any compunction about committing violence against a possible witness."

Erin nodded.

"Do you want to go back to sleep?"

"No. I think maybe I'll have a bath, see if it helps some of these aches."

"Sure. Are you finished with this tray?"

Erin uncovered her eyes and looked at it. She didn't have any more appetite for the meager breakfast. "Yes. I'm sorry, I'm just not ready to eat much yet today."

"That's fine." He picked up the tray from her lap so that she had the freedom to get out of bed for her bath.

CHAPTER 27

Terry was out during the afternoon. Erin ping-ponged around the house, a knot of anxiety in her stomach, looking for something to do, but unable to focus on anything. She cuddled with the animals and tempted Orange Blossom into chasing a string for a while but, eventually, he flopped over on his side, panting, and wouldn't pursue it anymore.

She flipped idly through one of Clementine's genealogy files but was unable to focus on it correctly. The names swam in front of her eyes, names that she was familiar with from Bald Eagle Falls, families who had raised children on the mountain for generations. They were all related, those who had been there for several generations.

Erin had checked the time half a dozen times during the afternoon. The clock seemed to be standing still. But finally, she heard the back door and knew that Vic was home.

"Erin? You up?"

"Upstairs."

Vic climbed the pull-down stairs to the attic. They usually visited in the kitchen or living room, Vic didn't have much occasion to be in the attic. She looked around and smiled. "So nice up here in your little hideaway." She sat down in the window seat, which looked toward her loft apartment over the garage. "So, how are you doing? You look a lot better than I expected."

"Just sore. Nothing particular, just an all-over ache. Like you get when you have the flu."

"You're lucky. Terry said the car was trashed."

"It rolled a few times."

"Sheesh. I'd at least expect a few bruises."

Erin nodded. "I don't know how I managed to get out without a scratch or visible bruises. The doctor said I need to watch out for any concussion symptoms. I guess even if you don't hit your head on something, your brain still bounces around inside your skull. But I've been okay. No dizziness or double-vision. Just sore and tired. A little distracted."

"Very lucky. I'm glad you won't be spending Christmas in the hospital."

"Me too."

Erin thought briefly about Christmas. They would have Christmas dinner together again, just like at Christmas the year before and Thanksgiving a few weeks previous. Aside from that, she didn't have any plans. She hoped she would just be able to relax and enjoy a day off without any expectations. She didn't have to fit in any religious rituals. She and Terry hadn't officially been together the previous year. She didn't know whether as well as their Christmas dinner together, he had also attended any mass or observance. Even people who didn't think about church all year long sometimes attended church at Christmas.

"So, what's your plan for the bake sale?" Vic inquired. "Are you going to be able to make it? We've got it covered, so you don't have to, but of course, you can if you want to."

"I've been going stir-crazy today. So I'd better!"

"Good. Always nice to have the face of Auntie Clem's Bakery there. People associate you with all of the good stuff you bake and will buy more if you're there."

Erin's face warmed at the compliment. She wasn't sure it was true. People knew her employees just as well as her, and maybe even better, since mostly they had been in Bald Eagle Falls longer than Erin had.

"I had really hoped that they would have the burglaries solved by now," Vic sighed. "It would be nice to have the fundraisers without the specter of more thefts hanging over our heads. How can people relax if they think that the new stuff might be stolen too?"

Erin thought about that. It wasn't just an idle worry. What if they raised a bunch of money and, since the burglars lived in Bald Eagle Falls, they knew where the money was kept and could steal that too. Or if they stole the new presents once they were purchased and the toys collected for the toy drive.

"We should do something to ensure that people can't," she said slowly. "I don't know if the police department has the resources to guard everything. Maybe we could set up a citizen's guard to keep an eye on things."

"How do we ensure that none of the guards are burglars? And then once the gifts go to the families they are intended for… even if we wait until Christmas Eve, how do we keep anyone from breaking in and stealing them on Christmas Eve, just like The Grinch?"

"Nobody could break into all of the houses on Christmas Eve. Maybe one or two if people were heavy sleepers, but everyone is going to be home that night. They're not going to find presents in empty houses."

"Except maybe during church services. There's a candlelight service Christmas Eve at First Baptist. I don't know what's going on at the other churches."

What would people choose when faced with the possibilities? Stay home to make sure their children had presents, or go to church services together? In some families, the father could stay home while the mother took the children to services, but not every family had two parents.

"We should talk to Terry or the sheriff about it, I guess. See if they have a plan."

They would have to come to a landing pretty quickly. The bake sale was the next day, and it was only a few days until Christmas.

~

Terry's eyes were even more tired than usual when he got home. It was late; he'd ended up putting in eight hours even though he wasn't supposed to be working full shifts.

He rubbed at the corners of his eyes, his skin looking thin and yellow. He had clearly done too much. He held up his hands in a 'stop' motion to Erin before she could open her mouth to say anything.

"Yes, I know I was gone too long and you're worried about me. And I'll tell you what I can, but before anything else, I need to sit down and put a cold pack on my head and a cold beer in my belly."

Erin turned and walked into the kitchen ahead of him. "You'll need more than beer. Have you had anything to eat?"

"The department sprang for pizza. So I didn't go hungry, but I've probably had too much caffeine. I needed something to keep me on my feet."

"You'd better not try to go to bed too early, then, but you can at least relax."

He sank into one of the kitchen chairs. "Believe me; I'm not planning to do anything else for the next twelve hours."

"Good."

She went to the fridge to provide him with the necessities and started the tea kettle heating for herself.

She didn't ask him all of the questions that were running through her mind. She wanted to know so much.

But he hadn't called or texted to let her know that they had caught the burglars, so she knew they were still in the same position as they had been at the beginning of the day. Even though she dreaded them interrogating Harold, she had hoped that something good would come of it. He would be able to provide them with the critical pieces of information that they needed to break the case.

Terry popped the tab on his beer and took a long pull. Erin got a doggie biscuit out of the cookie jar for K9. Orange Blossom's treat radar immediately pinged, and he was in the kitchen demanding to be fed. Marshmallow followed more sedately.

"Treats for everybody," Erin agreed, doling out the appropriate snacks to each of them. "Then you'll be quiet so that I can talk with Terry in peace."

Terry watched her, sipping on his beer, lounging back in his chair to stretch his fatigued back and shoulders. Erin finished handing out the treats, poured boiling water into her teacup, and sat down at the table with him.

"So… what happened? What can you tell me?"

"Not a lot, unfortunately. We've done our best with the potential witnesses, but people are not talking."

"Harold?"

"We had him in and did our best… but I think you got more out of him than we did."

Erin couldn't show him her reaction to this news, but she was both relieved that they hadn't broken Harold down and a bit proud that they hadn't been able to get any more information out of him than she had.

"So he didn't tell you anything?"

"No. Didn't confirm that it was anyone at school. Didn't want to tell us anything. Not obstructive, more… scared and shy, I think. Not nearly as easy to confide in a cop as a pretty lady he admires."

Erin's face burned. She looked away, trying to hide her reaction.

"Then his mother showed up and put an end to the questioning. No way I was bullying her child into confessing something he hadn't done."

Erin rolled her eyes. Of course, Terry wouldn't do that, but she herself had been worried about how the police would treat Harold. Not Terry, necessarily, but one of the others… Stayner, for instance.

"Well, I'm glad she was looking out for him, but I'm sorry you weren't able to get anywhere."

"Me too. I had hoped that by the end of the day, we would be able to say we had made some progress. Maybe even arrested some suspects. But as things stand now, we're not much further ahead than we were a day or two ago."

"You don't have anyone who looks good for it?"

"I have plenty of people who look good for it. But no one who fits exactly and no one that we have enough evidence to arrest and press charges against. If we could catch them red-handed with some of the loot, that would be ideal."

Erin nodded. She sipped her tea. It wasn't particularly tasty, but it was supposed to help her to sleep, and she wanted to be fresh for the next day.

"Have you thought about all of the money and gifts from the charity drives? They could be next." She set down her cup. "If it was me, that would be the best target. That's a lot of loot."

Terry stared at her for a minute. "Yeah. I wonder if we can capitalize on that. Make it a really attractive target and then catch them at it."

Erin raised her brows. Maybe there was something they could do other than just protecting the gifts. She hadn't thought about using it as bait.

"It would be really nice to get these guys."

"Yes, it would."

CHAPTER 28

Then it was the day of the bake sale. Erin's baking was all prepared, and everything had been stored in the school kitchens. She opened Auntie Clem's for the morning, but closed at noon and Bella drove her over to the school. A couple of her employees had been sent over earlier to set everything up, so when she got there, there wasn't a lot left to do. She looked everything over, made sure it was all clearly labeled, and set up her cash box so she could make change quickly.

She wasn't as sore as she had been the day after the accident, but she was still pretty tender and wasn't able to stand for long periods. She was given a chair and did most of her transactions sitting down, developing a crick in her neck from looking up at everyone.

It was busy, and sales were brisk. The bake sale, book sale, and a table for the toy drive were all set up in the gymnasium. There were lots of smiles and Merry Christmas wishes going around. Erin saw Harold across the gym, but he didn't approach her table or talk to her. She watched to see if he was there with any of his friends, or if she could catch any interactions—positive or nega-tive—with other boys from the school. But she saw that Mrs. Melville was going to each of the charity tables. Harold was standing there waiting for her to finish, probably with strict instructions not to move from the spot.

When Mrs. Melville arrived at Erin's table, she did not smile. Erin wondered whether Harold had told her about Erin's inquiries, or whether she blamed Erin for Officer Piper's actions, or whether she was just sour-faced and unhappy because of the stress of the season and everything that had been going on in Bald Eagle Falls. It couldn't be easy for the family as newcomers to the area. It was easier to blame the outsiders for the burglaries than it was to blame the people you had lived next door to and trusted for years, so they had probably been under the microscope.

"Hello, Mrs. Melville," Erin said as cheerfully as she could, hoping to pass some good feelings on to the woman.

Mrs. Melville still did not crack a smile. She gave a curt nod but did not answer Erin. She picked up one of Mrs. Hadrian's banana loaves and a plate of cookies. She did not touch Erin's gluten-free Grinches, which meant that Harold would not be able to partake of any of the bake sale treats. She counted out a few coins and bills and managed to come up with exact change for the purchases, which she handed to Erin, then gathered up her goods and walked away without a word.

"Somebody got up on the wrong side of the bed," Bella commented in a low voice.

Erin glanced over at her and didn't answer. Bella knew better than to be making comments about the customers, especially when there were still other customers around. No one wanted to think that people were talking about them behind their backs.

She tried to catch Harold's eye to at least nod to him, but he avoided looking in her direction. Erin sighed and continued to smile and greet people and encourage everyone she could to buy the baked goods and donate to the cause.

～

There was a sudden increase in chatter, and Erin looked up from her transaction with Mrs. Peach to see what was going on. She saw a Santa across the gym from them. Erin looked over at Bella.

"I didn't know they were going to do Santa today, did you?"

Bella shook her head. "I never heard it announced. Maybe they decided to do something for the little kids…"

Erin looked around, waiting for an announcement to be made. The school telling the kids there to line up if they wanted to each get a visit with Santa. But none of the school administrators were coming forward to pick up the mike. They seemed just as surprised as anybody else to find Santa in their midst.

Erin watched the kids crowd around Santa, all calling out and trying to get his attention, tugging on his clothes and speaking over each other.

Santa gave a few 'ho ho ho's' and 'Merry Christmases' and attempted to walk across the gym without tripping over all of the little rug rats trying to get his attention. He moved in abbreviated steps, cajoling them.

"Santa just wanted to have a look around, see how all of the fundraising is going," he told them, trying to shake them all off.

Erin didn't recognize the Santa's voice. She watched him make slow progress across the gym.

"Everybody is being such good helpers to Santa," Santa said. "Can you kids be good helpers too and let Santa go for a few minutes? I want to get a head start on some Christmas cookies. Santa needs to train too, you know. You think I can go all year without eating cookies and then be able to eat all of the cookies you leave out for me on Christmas Eve?"

"I thought you burned it off," one of the kids piped up authoritatively. "Because you have to do so much work all in one night. With magic and going all the way around the world and leaving presents for everyone. That burns a lot of calories."

"I still need to train," Santa insisted, patting his stomach. He made it to the bake sale table and looked at the goodies spread across the table. He nodded at Erin.

She had assumed she would recognize whoever it was, but she still didn't know the eyes framed by the beard and hat.

He gave her a wink with one of his cheerful blue eyes. "There seem to be an awful lot of Grinches around here," he observed, looking at the green cookies Erin and Vic had made.

"We've had a lot of Grinches in Bald Eagle Falls lately," Erin said, studying what little of his face she could see, along with his body language and demeanor. If he was one of the burglars, she would certainly not have guessed it by the way he talked and moved. He didn't seem to be at all concerned about being watched. With every eye in the place on him, he wouldn't be able to get away with anything.

"And how are you feeling, Miss Erin?"

Erin shifted uncomfortably, looking up at him. She pushed herself to her feet so that she at least didn't have to strain her neck to look at him. She didn't like a stranger calling her Miss Erin, acting like Erin should know who he was. She glanced at Vic, trying to get a read on the situation. Was she overreacting to the Santa's presence? Was it expected, or should she be worried about it? Vic raised her brows and didn't seem to have the answer.

"Who are you?" she asked in a low voice. Maybe it was somebody that she ought to know. She was just confused by the beard.

"I'm Santa Claus," he said cheerfully. "Kris Kringle. The fat guy. Whatever you like."

She looked down at the cookies. "So what can I get you today? You don't like the Grinches?"

"I'll take a Grinch. Always wanted to bite his head off. And some banana bread, and…" He surveyed the rest of the table. "Are those tarts yours?"

Erin nodded. "Yes, the pumpkin. Those are ours."

"And you made them yourself?"

"Yes."

"I hear a lot of cats like pumpkin."

The hair on Erin's arms stood up.

Cats?

Was that supposed to be a threat?

Or was he saying that he was the one who had poisoned Orange Blossom, that it wasn't just a freak accident? She was pretty sure that pumpkin was just fine for cats. It wasn't on the list of things that Doc had told her to look for at her house.

"I… don't know. Do they?" she asked uncertainly.

"Yes. Doesn't your cat like pumpkin?"

"I don't know. I never fed any to him."

"You ought to try it sometime."

Was it possible that he had poisoned Orange Blossom? That he had hidden some kind of poison in a pumpkin dish and then coaxed Blossom to eat it? But how would he have gotten into the house?

None of the houses had been damaged in the break-ins. No broken windows or doors. Whoever was doing the stealing knew a thing or two about breaking into a house, even one with a burglar alarm. Erin's system had been foiled once before and, though that weak point had been corrected, there was always the possibility of some other vulnerability.

"Now, don't do anything that would put you on the naughty list," Santa warned Erin. "You wouldn't want to get moved off of the nice list and get a lump of coal on Christmas morning."

Was Santa implying that he would burn her house down? Or was it just some Christmas silliness?

Vic moved closer to Erin and the Santa, her movements taking on a certain wary intensity that told Erin she was now on full alert and wasn't about to put up with any nonsense from the Santa.

The Santa put a Grinch cookie, banana bread loaf, and pumpkin tarts in front of Erin and patted his red suit pockets until he found his wallet. Erin rang it up and told him his total, then took his proffered twenty.

"No change," Santa said, a twinkle in his eye. "We want to help as many kids as we can, don't we?" He picked up the bag of baking and turned to make his way back across the gym, kids starting to pester him again. He boomed plenty of 'Merry Christmases' and 'ho ho ho's' and made his way out of the gym.

"Do you know who that was?" Erin asked Bella, her heart pounding hard.

"I think it might have been Mr. Hopewell," Bella offered. "But I can't be sure. I don't know him really well. He's new here. He's the junior science teacher, so I don't have any classes with him."

After the sale was finished and the doors were closed, Erin and the others gathered their money and donations to total everything and see how they had done. Husbands and boyfriends stood around at the doors to the gym to make sure that no one could take them unaware and make off with the cash. Terry was there, as well as Willie, Naomi's husband, Beaver and Jeremy, the sheriff, and Tom Baker. Everyone determined to make sure that the donations would make it to the intended parties.

"Did you see the Howie boys hanging around in the hall outside the gym?" Vic asked Erin. "Their family was one of those that was hit. I guess at least the older ones know that they aren't getting anything for Christmas unless people are generous at the fundraisers."

Erin had noticed them loitering nearby. Families in Bald Eagle Falls tended to have larger families than those in the city or farther north in the urban areas Erin had lived in. The Howies had at least six boys.

"I hope the younger ones don't know what happened. It would be nice if they didn't know how close they came to losing their Christmas. At that age… it would be nice for them just to enjoy the anticipation of a special day."

Vic nodded, her eyes shiny. "We never had a whole lot for Christmas, but it was always a special time. I guess I knew pretty early on that there wasn't any Santa Claus coming down our chimney. I don't remember a time when I didn't know that the presents came from Pa and Mom. We knew how hard they worked, and anything special was… that much more special."

Erin finished counting and stacking all of her bills and moved on to the coins. "We did really well. I think we'll be on track to give all of the families who were burglarized and all of the ones who were supposed to be getting something from the needy children's fund a nice day."

"Good." Vic breathed out in relief. "And that's just us. With the toy drive and the book sale as well, and whatever other fundraisers are wrapping up today… this town has really come together. Everybody deserves a pat on the back."

"Almost everybody," Erin amended, thinking about the burglars.

"Yeah, everybody except the ones who stole everything in the first place," Vic agreed. "Somehow, I don't see *those* Grinches skiing down the mountain to return everyone's things when they come to understand the true meaning of Christmas."

Erin laughed. "No, I don't think so."

CHAPTER 29

There were more children than usual playing outside the school when Erin left the building, closely escorted by Terry, who was determined to make sure that nothing further happened to her and she was able to deposit the money and get home unmolested. Since school had let out early, she had expected the schoolyard to be quieter. Everyone would be going home to tend to their own Christmas preparations, play with friends, or whatever else they liked to do away from the school.

But children bounced balls in the basketball court where Harold had been playing the night of the fundraising meeting. Others ran playing tag or sat on benches or makeshift seats while they looked at their phones and tapped out messages to each other. There were children with their parents and other friends who tagged along with them while their own parents worked or shopped or ran errands.

She watched them, and they watched her making her way to Terry's truck. Did they all know what had happened to her? That she had been forced off the road and could have died? How many of them knew why or who it was? The way that rumors were flying around at the school, there had to be children who knew.

She didn't see any sign of any Santas in the parking lot.

Terry gave Erin a hand up into the truck, though she was quite capable of climbing up into the cab herself. He took a careful look around, studying the various groups of children and analyzing threats and group dynamics. He looked up at Erin before shutting the door.

"It will all be okay," Erin told him.

His face was grim as he nodded agreement. Like he had to agree because it was in the script he'd been given, but he didn't really buy into it. He was tired. It had been another long, fatiguing day. He was putting in too many hours and he wasn't going to be able to get caught up on his sleep on the holiday.

He slammed her door shut, and Erin waited there while he went around to his side and climbed up into the driver's seat after sending K9 into the back.

"Now is the time to be careful," he warned. "I don't want you to think that it's a home run because we made good money at the bake sale. We need to keep the money safe like you said yesterday."

"I know. That's why I'm here with you. I'm not going off somewhere on my own."

He showed his teeth in a smile. "There might be a good side to having your car totaled. Now that you can't get around on your own, I can keep better track of you."

"I never hid where I was from you."

"And I never tracked you. But I also never expected you to be targeted like that. By someone who fully intended to kill you because you might know something about the burglaries."

Erin couldn't help shivering with the cold wave that washed over her. She wanted to object that Terry couldn't know what their intention was.

Perhaps they had only intended to warn her, to scare her.

But she knew it wasn't true.

The brick through the window had been a warning. She had disregarded it, telling herself it was just some sort of prank or mistake, and had gone on to talk to Harold. Then they had ramped up the consequences and done their best to kill her.

And Orange Blossom? Had that been a warning? And the Santa at the bake sale? Had he been warning her off or just making jokes?

She didn't say anything as they drove to the bank. Terry put his hand on her arm to prevent her from getting out, looking around to make sure there was nothing that triggered suspicions. Then he nodded. "I'll walk you to the door."

"Are you sure you don't want to walk me all the way to the counter? I don't think anyone is going to do anything in the parking lot with you right here!"

"I don't either. But I wouldn't have expected anyone would run you off the road, either, and they did. We haven't yet found the truck that did it. It's got to have some front end damage. But there's no sign of it around town."

"They probably took it into the city to have it fixed."

"Or dumped it in a river somewhere. There are lots of good places to abandon vehicles out here."

"But you'd know from the VIN number, wouldn't you? If you ever found it, you'd know whose it was."

"Could be stolen. Though I haven't had any stolen vehicle reports either. But they don't always come in right away."

Erin climbed out of the truck.

"Why would anyone not report a vehicle theft right away? They'd end up in trouble with the police and their insurance agency then, wouldn't they?" she asked.

He walked around the truck to meet her and take her to the door. "People don't always know when a vehicle has been stolen."

At Erin's doubtful look, he raised his eyebrows. "Where is your other vehicle?"

"At the junkyard." Then she realized he'd said *other* vehicle and had to think about what he meant. "Oh… you mean Clementine's car? It's in the garage."

"When is the last time you saw it?"

"I don't know. It's been a while, but…"

"Would you know if someone had taken it?"

"If someone broke into the garage? I would know."

"How?"

"We would have heard them. The door would be open. Someone would have tipped us off. Like Mrs. Peach calling me to tell me that there was a hole in my window."

"And if it was done covertly? Someone picked the lock on the side door, hit the garage door opener switch, and drove the car out? If they closed everything again when they were done, would you know the difference? How long would it take before you reported the theft of your vehicle?"

Erin paused at the door with him. "I don't think I've been in there for months. Only a couple of times since the garage was built. And then… just to put something into storage."

"It's easy to lose track of your possessions if you don't see them very often. And some folks around here have more cars than they know what to do with. You have a half a dozen kids, and you end up needing more than one or two cars for Mom and Dad. Or you retire and buy a luxury car, but you still have the old beater to fall back on. And farm vehicles. And maybe something that you're holding on to for the collector in the family when he gets old enough to drive or to work on it. One family, out on a farm with plenty of space, might end up with six different vehicles. And if one of them disappears, nobody really thinks anything about it."

"I guess so. I never thought of that." Erin walked into the bank and stood in line, pondering over what Terry had said. The reverse would also be true. A family with half a dozen vehicles might not even notice if another one was added to their stables. Park the car in question on someone else's property, pull a tarp over it, and they might not even notice it in their daily comings and goings. The truck that had driven her off the road could be anywhere, hidden or in plain sight, and all she could say was that it was a big, dark pickup truck. There had to be hundreds of them in the county. Everyone had a pickup truck.

The cashiers were waiting for Erin and the other ladies who had been involved in the charity drives. One of them motioned Erin over as soon as she walked into the bank. "Over here, Miss Price. I'll take you now."

Erin looked at the other people standing in line who had gotten there ahead of her. "I can wait…"

"No, you can't. You have an appointment. Come on."

Erin walked up to the counter and smiled at the young woman who was waiting for her. She didn't know Paige Chesterton very well, but she knew her on sight, and Paige had always been very pleasant toward her.

Out of the corner of her eye, she saw movement and a flash of red, and she knew before she finished turning her head what she was going to see. A man in a Santa suit, of course, though he had a coat pulled on over top of the suit that had kept her from noticing him the minute she walked into the bank.

Her heart raced. She stood there frozen, the deposit bag in her hand, trying to figure out what to do if he made a sudden dash toward her or pulled a weapon.

The Santa turned his head to look in her direction. He wasn't wearing his beard. Probably people weren't allowed to go into the bank with their faces obscured. It was just Willie. Erin hadn't even known that he was doing any Santa gigs. Not that he told her everything he did; she had just never thought to ask.

Willie gave Erin a nod and a little salute, and took a look around the bank. He nodded a couple of times quickly, indicating that everything looked safe.

With Terry watching for trouble outside and Willie inside, Erin was finally able to relax. She rolled her sore shoulders and set the deposit bag down on the counter.

She smiled at Paige. "Okay. I just need to make a deposit for the bake sale funds. I want to make sure that the money is safe until it can be used as we promised."

"We don't want any mishaps," Paige agreed cheerfully. Despite her smile and cheer, she looked around the bank carefully, as if marking each person who was there. Her eyes lingered for a moment on Terry, standing outside the door keeping his eyes open. Then she smiled at Erin again, nodding. "Have you filled out a deposit slip? Good. If you'll wait while I re-count the money and verify the amount…"

She didn't have one of the fancy machines for counting money like some of the big banks Erin had been to. She just carefully counted it up by hand, adding together all of the totals of each kind of bill together, then counting the pile of change. She verified Erin's total with a smile, and carefully put everything into a drawer with a slot in the front.

"All done," she said. "Thank you for choosing to bank with us."

It wasn't like there were a lot of banks in Bald Eagle Falls to choose from. Erin smiled, thanked Paige, and turned back toward the door. Outside, she couldn't help mirroring Terry's actions, looking around for anyone suspicious, feeling anxious that nothing had happened and feeling like the burglars might come in at any moment to hold the bank up at gunpoint.

She laughed at herself for being so dramatic, drawing Terry's attention to her. He smiled and nodded, acknowledging the ridiculousness of the situation. "That's the bake sale money safe. The sheriff will make sure that the book drive money is deposited safely. Then it's just a matter of keeping the toy drive donations safe. And a few smaller fundraisers that won't make very much."

"Do you think they will be safe? Do you think the burglars will attempt to steal all of the toys again?"

Terry sighed. "I know it sounds silly and dramatic, but… yes, I have to say, I don't think they'll be able to resist the temptation."

~

Erin was exhausted at the end of the day. Her body was sore, not yet recovered from the accident. She was used to being on her feet all day at the bakery, but even having sat most of the time at the bake sale, she collapsed on her bed when she was finally home.

"A long day?" Terry suggested.

"Yeah. I feel like I ran a marathon. Or the whole Iron Man thing. I don't know when I've been so tired and sore."

"You did too much."

"Maybe," Erin admitted. "But I'm glad I was there. I wouldn't have wanted to miss it."

"Yeah." Terry nodded understandingly. "Well, nothing bad happened, and you can spend the rest of the day relaxing."

"Oh…" Erin realized she had not yet told him about the strange encounter with the Santa at the school.

"Oh?" Terry repeated.

"I just… before I forget… who knows if I'll remember to tell you later."

She filled him in on the Santa situation at the school, and then about the scare Willie had given her at the bank. Terry chuckled.

"Now you'll be seeing Santas wherever you go. Oh, wait a minute… there *are* Santas everywhere you go."

She pretended to punch him in the arm. "You're a big help!"

"I'll look into him," Terry assured her. "We're screening everyone we can at the school, but it's hard when you know so little about who might be involved. I'll move Mr. Hopewell up the list. Just to be sure."

"Yeah. It's probably nothing. I just… I don't want to ignore any… red flags."

Terry nodded his agreement. He suggested supper, but Erin shook her head. "You go ahead and scrounge up something for yourself. I'm not hungry, just tired. I'm going to go to sleep."

"Are you sure I can't get you something? I'll make you whatever you like."

"No. Thanks. Maybe I'll take you up on the offer tomorrow."

She closed her eyes. Terry stood there looking down at her for a minute, then quietly left the bedroom. Erin could hear his footsteps as he entered the kitchen and then remembered nothing more.

lthough she was tired, she slept restlessly. She kept waking up and turning over, trying to find the sweet spot in her bed and to get back to sleep. Her body was so sore that, like when she had the flu, she couldn't stay in one position for any length of time. The bouncing and stretching as the car had rolled over must have really put a strain on her muscles and joints.

She rubbed her eyes, pounded her pillow, and tried to find a deeper sleep. She felt beside her, but Terry's half of the bed was empty. He was either still up, or had been in bed and gotten back up again. Since he had been attacked, he'd had a much harder time sleeping. He often got up and watched TV until he could drop off, sometimes coming back to bed once he was drowsy and sometimes just passing out on the couch.

Erin thought of calling him. If they were both trying to get to sleep, then maybe they could cuddle and comfort each other and help each other to get to sleep. But she knew that the opposite was more likely to happen, with each of them rousing the other as they moved restlessly and tossed from one side to the other. If he'd fallen asleep in front of the TV, then it was better just to let him sleep there.

As Erin drifted from awake to restless sleep, her mind

wandered, her dreams jumping from one time and place to another in a chaotic collage.

"Terry?" she called out, feeling for him again. But he wasn't there. Erin snuggled down, looking for a deeper sleep.

"They're gone! The presents are gone!"

Erin squinted and looked around, trying to figure out who was talking. Her mind was restless and she couldn't quite wake up.

"Which presents?" she mumbled. "I didn't buy any presents."

"The ones that are most needed," a hearty man's voice told her. She tried to figure out who it was. Vice Principal Fitzroy? Or maybe the voice of some actor she had seen on TV. It all felt a little bit like she was in a movie on TV. Removed and surreal. She couldn't remember where she had heard that voice.

"The needy children's donations?" she suggested.

"Need and want. Ignorance and want. Are there no prisons?"

Erin tried to compute this. Something was niggling away there in the back of her brain. She had heard it all before. Why? Where had it come from?

"We did everything we could to replace the toys," she informed the voice. "We've been holding fundraisers to replace what was stolen, and everybody has been contributing, even if they could only manage a dollar or two. People have really come together."

"It isn't enough. We must help the children."

"Okay. I will. In the morning. We don't have much time."

"Time? The time is drawing near. Tonight at midnight."

Erin startled in her sleep and woke herself up. The words stuck in her brain.

Tonight at midnight.

She tried to go back to sleep again, feeling for the dream she had been having. It had been an uncomfortable dream, but at least she had been able to sleep. She wanted to get back to that place again.

Her brain would not cooperate. Erin got up and wandered to the commode. If she just walked for a moment, relieved herself, and had a glass of water, maybe she would be able to return to sleep like she had never left it. She didn't care if it was the same dream or not, as long as she could sleep.

But after the bathroom, she was more wide awake than ever. She traipsed to the living room to see if Terry was asleep. He was either still awake or had been awakened by her wandering.

"Erin? Are you okay?"

"It's okay; I'm just… I can't sleep. I had a dream…"

He straightened up. "Was it *the* dream?"

The dream where she kept finding Mr. Inglethorpe's body over and over again, changing identity every time and appearing there as one of her friends or acquaintances.

"No. It was something different. Not a nightmare, just… confused."

He made space beside himself for her. Erin sat down and cuddled up to him, hoping her body would settle down and figure out that she still needed more sleep.

"Tonight at midnight," she murmured.

"What's that?"

"That's what the man in my dream said. That it would be tonight at midnight. I think he meant that's when the presents will be stolen." She yawned widely, trying to cover her mouth with her hand.

Terry turned his wrist to look at his watch. It lit up. "It's already past midnight," he said. "I haven't had any call that the presents have been stolen or that any attempt was made."

Erin shook her head. "So much for the prognosticating power of dreams. Can't even get the time right."

"If you just had the dream, then maybe it means *tonight* at midnight."

Erin closed her eyes. "Maybe it does," she agreed.

"If it was me, I wouldn't want to wait for long. I wouldn't want to wait until the last minute. Especially not until Christmas Eve when people will be home with their families."

"Yeah."

"And it makes sense to wait until after the bake sale money has been used to buy gifts. They weren't able to steal it before it was deposited, so they missed out on that opportunity. So now there wouldn't be as big a haul. If I were the burglar," Terry paused, considering, "I would want to hit it when it was as much loot as possible. After all of the gifts are bought, but before they are distributed."

"Then we should do something about that. We shouldn't get everything and then wait until Christmas Eve to give them all out. We should start the distribution today. Start putting together the gifts for the family groups that we already have enough for and delivering them." Get the loot split up as quickly as we can.

In the darkness, she could feel Terry nodding his head slowly. "Yes… that's not a bad idea. It makes the families more vulnerable than if we deliver the gifts on Christmas Eve, but spreading the gifts around makes it more difficult for the burglars to target everything. They'll have to prioritize their targets, and it will take longer, give us more opportunities to catch them."

"Right."

"Not a bad idea, Miss Price. Not bad at all."

Erin had fallen back asleep on the couch cuddled up to Terry, which meant that she woke up with a crick in her neck that wouldn't go away. She had known she wouldn't be able to put in a full day at the bakery after her difficulties at the bake sale the day before, so she allowed Bella and Vic to run things at the bakery and went with Terry to the police department in the town center to help sort the items donated to the toy drive and figure out what they still needed to buy. She was able to sit and rest when she needed to and she chatted with Terry or with Clara during her breaks. She and Clara had never gotten along well, but Erin could make small talk and be pleasant, which was all that was required. Clara had no overwhelming desire for them to be buddies.

"Are you up to Christmas shopping?" Terry asked, looking in on Erin while she sat resting, drinking a glass of water.

"If you give me a few more minutes to rest, I'll be fine. I can do things, but just for a little bit at a time."

"Can you rest in the truck while I drive to the city?"

"Are we going all the way into the city to shop?"

"I figure they'll have better selection and pricing than out here. It costs extra to get stuff shipped to Bald Eagle Falls, so you always pay a premium in town."

"Okay. Let's go into the city, then. But I might sleep in the truck."

"Sure. That's fine with me. Maybe I'll have a nap too."

Erin glared at him dramatically. "You better not!"

"If you can, why can't I?" he teased.

"Because your eyes are supposed to be on the road." She faked punching him in the shoulder.

He smiled, the dimple appearing in his cheek. "Oh, that's right…"

Erin was glad that he was in good spirits.

CHAPTER 31

*E*rin slept both on the way to the city to do the shopping and on the way back. Her body ached and the crick in her neck did not get better with sleeping in the truck. But she was happy with what they had been able to buy with the bake sale money, and she and Terry agreed that he would start delivering the completed family packages immediately.

Before Terry took the gifts back to the police department, he dropped Erin off at Auntie Clem's Bakery so that she could check in with her employees and make sure that everything was going well.

Vic and Bella were all smiles, cheerfully relating the various customers who had been in during the day. While she would have preferred to have been there in person, Erin enjoyed hearing the secondhand stories.

"Oh, and here's Mary Lou," Vic said, looking toward the door. Erin turned around to see Mary Lou Cox coming toward the bakery. Erin smiled and nodded a greeting. Mary Lou did not return the smile as she came in the door. Erin felt a little disconcerted. She was at a disadvantage. She should have been on the other side of the counter, serving customers, not chatting from the customer side. It felt strange to be there when Mary Lou came by.

Mary Lou stood just inside the door, not advancing the rest of the way up to the display case and order counter. Erin swallowed, looking at her grim expression.

"What is it? Has something happened?"

Mary Lou pressed her lips together. "That's an interesting question for you to ask."

"Well, I mean, I know about the burglaries of course, if that's what you mean. And I guess you heard about my car accident." She looked for anything that Mary Lou might be upset about. "I didn't see you at the bake sale yesterday. We've already been out buying some new gifts, but if you wanted to make a donation, I'm sure we could—"

"I am not here to donate to the bake sale fund. I'm here because of what you have done, interfering in our lives. After all that we have been through, I thought that you understood."

Erin swallowed. Her chest was tight and there was a feeling of dread in the pit of her stomach. "I'm not sure what you're upset about, Mary Lou, but if you tell me, I'll try to straighten it out…"

"After all that my family has gone through the past few years, I thought that people would give us a break. Instead, you sic the police on Joshua."

"Me? I didn't…" Erin trailed off, remembering how she had told Terry about Harold's question. *You know about them?*

Mary Lou's eyes burned. She took in Erin's sudden silence and how she didn't deny the accusation. She nodded her head. "Exactly. You're the one who accused Joshua. How could you?"

"I didn't. That's not what happened. I didn't accuse him of anything, I just… I repeated what someone else had said, a question, not an accusation. You know that they think the burglars are at the school, that's where the police have been focusing their efforts…"

"Joshua is not one of the burglars."

"I'm sure he isn't. It wasn't an accusation. Just a throwaway comment, but it was bothering me, and I asked Terry…"

"And Officer Piper is part of the police force in Bald Eagle

Falls. You can't separate your pillow talk from an official report. For your Officer Piper, it's all the same. You can't say something like that to him without him investigating it."

Erin covered up her mouth, hiding her grimace. "I didn't mean for him to investigate Joshua. Everybody is under scrutiny. I don't think that it was Joshua."

"You think that he's a criminal. That both him and Campbell are mixed up in crime, because of what happened over Thanksgiving. But that wasn't Campbell's fault. And it was nothing at all to do with Joshua. You should be ashamed of yourself for repeating gossip and throwing accusations around so recklessly."

Erin bit her lip, trying to keep her emotions under control. It had been a hard enough week without Mary Lou accusing her of wrongdoing on top of everything else.

"Erin doesn't think that Joshua is a criminal," Vic piped up. "You know she's been right there to support you all through everything that happened with Campbell. She never accused him of anything and did her best to help prove he was innocent. She put herself in danger helping Joshua. Why would she turn around and accuse him of something?"

Mary Lou frowned and shook her head, her brows drawing down. "Put herself in danger? What are you talking about?"

Erin looked at Vic. Vic's mouth hung open as she tried to figure out how to take back what had slipped out of her mouth.

Mary Lou looked from one to the other. "Erin, what is Vic talking about? When did you put yourself in danger helping Joshua? Why don't I know anything about this?"

"Uh…"

"Tell me what's going on."

"I thought you knew," Vic said, putting both hands on top of her head like she was afraid it was going to explode. "Didn't Beaver…?"

"Beaver?"

"Oh, shoot. Shoot, shoot, shoot…"

Mary Lou put her hands on her hips. "One of you had better start explaining."

Erin rubbed her temples and tried to downplay it. "Joshua went into the city. He and Jeremy. When Brianna was missing. They were trying to find her."

"Oh?"

"Yes…" Vic agreed, "And… Erin and I ran into them, just by accident, and we kind of joined up to help them. Erin didn't want them to search for Brianna. She tried to talk them out of it. But we all said that we were going ahead, so she said she'd come along too."

"And…?"

"And… well… things didn't go exactly the way we had thought they would. And we ended up dealing with some pretty nasty characters. Erin was the only one who had the sense to know that we were doing something stupid. We just thought we would talk to people, and if we ran into any problems, we were armed, so…"

"Armed?" Mary Lou repeated faintly, moving farther into the bakery and putting her hand on one of the chairs to steady herself. "Joshua was armed?"

"No, not Joshua. But… me and Jeremy. And we thought that we could handle any trouble."

"You are children! What made you think you could take on thugs with guns?"

"We're not children," Vic protested, her face turning red. To Mary Lou, they were. They were only a couple of years older than her boys. Even if they were technically adults, she didn't see them that way.

"So… don't get after Erin. She knows Joshua isn't a criminal."

Mary Lou looked at Erin, studying her closely. Erin couldn't hold her gaze. She hoped that Joshua wasn't involved in any of the burglaries, but she knew that other boys at the school were, and she couldn't automatically discount Joshua just because she liked him and had helped him out in the past. She couldn't assume that because she liked Mary Lou, that automatically meant that Joshua couldn't be involved in something criminal. Campbell, after all, had been involved with drug dealers and other bad stuff in the city. She didn't know if he was a user, or just an informant for Beaver, or if he had been more deeply involved in the drug trade.

Mary Lou shook her head. "You stay away from Joshua," she warned Erin. "I don't want you involved with him. Or you, Miss Victoria. And if you happen to see Beaver before I do, you can tell her in no uncertain terms that I don't want her involved with Josh either. It's bad enough that she involved Campbell in her investigations. Maybe he would have gotten involved in that life without her help, but I can't say that for sure. You can all just stay away from him and let him live his own life. He is *not* involved in these burglaries."

Erin nodded. "Yes. Okay."

Vic was still bright red. She indicated her agreement as well. Mary Lou's eyes went to Bella. Erin knew that she and Joshua were not friends, but that they at least knew each other. They both attended the same school and, in a small town like Bald Eagle Falls, the students quickly got to know each other.

Mary Lou didn't say anything to Bella. She turned and walked back out of the bakery.

Bella let out a breath. "Wow."

"I'm sorry," Vic said to Erin, her words coming out in a rush. "I should have kept my big mouth shut. I just made things worse. I'm so sorry."

"Don't worry about it. She should know what's been going on with Joshua. Someone should have told her before this."

CHAPTER 32

The school had involved the students in making cards and some paper decorations for the Christmas packages. They wouldn't know which families their cards were going to, so there were no names on them, but it was a nice way to get the students involved in the project and thinking about others who might be having a tough time during the holiday season.

Erin circulated the gymnasium, helping to supervise the effort and make sure that the finished cards were collected and sorted for them to be matched up with the family packages. She kept an eye out for any fat men in red suits, but there didn't seem to be any Santas around this time. Erin stopped near one of the groups of students, bunched close together to talk to each other while they drew or wrote. Peter Foster looked up from the card that he was working on and grinned at her.

"Hi, Miss Erin!"

"Hi, Peter. How's it coming along?"

"Pretty good." He sat back and looked at the card he had been working on. "It's Santa's sleigh, full of presents. I'm not a very good artist. The reindeer look kind of like dogs."

Erin laughed. "Well, maybe he decided to use dogs like Max in *The Grinch*."

Peter brightened. "Yeah! They can be dogs like Max. The antlers are just tied on." He carefully drew a string from the former reindeer's antlers to his chin and examined it again. "That's pretty good."

"Good job. I'm sure whoever gets it will like it."

Peter nodded. "I like dogs. Do you?"

"Sure. I like most animals."

"But you don't have a dog, you have a cat."

"Yes, that's right," Erin agreed, surprised that he knew this. "Orange Blossom. Isn't that a funny name for a cat?"

"And he got sick. That's what I heard." He looked at her questioningly.

"Yes, he did," Erin agreed. Small town gossip was certainly living up to its reputation.

"I was sorry he got sick."

"Me too. But he's doing better now."

"That's good." Peter continued to color. Then he put his crayon down and looked around at the other students and lowered his voice. "It's really sad about the kids who had their presents stolen. Nobody is telling us whose were stolen, but if they don't just have really little kids, if they have bigger kids like me, then the big kids know if their presents got stolen. So I know who some of them are." He shook his head. "It's very sad," he repeated. "And the needy kids' presents… why would anyone do that? They knew that those things were going to kids whose families couldn't afford anything for Christmas. Why would they steal from people who didn't have anything?"

"I don't know. I don't understand what they were thinking. I guess they just felt entitled to take them and didn't care who they hurt. We've been able to raise enough money that those kids can still have something for Christmas, so maybe they feel like they didn't cause any harm. But it's made things hard for a lot of people this Christmas."

She crouched down next to Peter, looking at his card and

getting closer to him so that other people wouldn't hear their conversation as easily.

"A lot of people who have given money and donations to replace the stolen presents didn't have very much to start with, so it's made it really tight. They won't be giving as much to their own kids, because they gave something up to help someone else."

"That's really good. Some people *are* good."

"Yes. Some people are really good."

"I don't like what the burglars are doing. Someone should tell them that what they are doing is wrong, even if the kids do still get presents for Christmas."

"I think they already know that what they are doing is wrong. They knew that from the start. But I wish that the people who know who it is would turn them in. It's not right that they're being protected by the people who know who they are."

Peter looked at Erin, frowning. "But you're supposed to do things that are good for your school, and not talk bad about the other students. That's school spirit."

"It's not school spirit to cover up for people you know are doing something wrong. That hurts everyone as much as the people who are doing the stealing."

"But the coach says if you have school spirit, you support your school and you don't do anything that might…" Peter searched his memory for the right word, "that might *detract* from the school's image."

"Keeping quiet about who is stealing things from other families is not showing school spirit. It's the opposite, because instead of people thinking you come from a school that teaches kids to be honest and good and to stand up for the right, they will think you come from a bad school that condones theft and dishonesty."

Peter nudged and elbowed a couple of the boys in his group. They looked at each other and at Erin, exchanging looks.

"Coach says we need to support our teams."

∾

For what seemed like a long time, Erin just crouched there, looking at Peter and analyzing his words and the looks that passed between the boys. She went over everything Peter had said and then started over again.

"Does the coach know who is doing the stealing?" she asked carefully.

Peter looked at one of the other boys for assistance. Erin remembered the same kinds of looks passing between Harold and his friends as they weighed what to say to her.

Erin's body ached and crouching down was aggravating too many muscles. She abandoned her position, leaning back and landing on her butt and stretching her legs out in front of her. She leaned over closer to the boys.

"Coach Hadrian knows who it is?" she whispered.

They didn't answer, but in her mind, Erin kept hearing what Peter had said about the coach.

We need to support our teams.

Had he been telling them—or been telling someone—that saying who the burglars were would be betraying their teams? Betraying the school? That meant, then, that there were boys on the team who were helping to commit the burglaries. They were known to Coach Hadrian, and he was actively trying to prevent them from being discovered.

Why would he be trying to prevent them from being discovered?

He didn't believe, like the little boys did, that he would be detracting from the image of the school if he didn't reveal who was breaking the law. He had to know that the entire school was going to be painted with the same brush if people came to understand that the burglars were students there.

She pretended to be looking at Peter's Christmas card, but she was scanning the rest of the gym, looking at the teachers and other adults who were milling around supervising. She picked up the card and used it for cover as she looked past it to see where the coach was, if he was there in the gym.

And he was.

He was standing just a few paces away from her.

His dark, intense eyes drilled into her, watching her intently.

CHAPTER 33

 rin swallowed. Her mouth was dry.

The toys had not been brought to the school, so there were no police guards close by keeping an eye on things. Just teachers who—she hoped—knew nothing about what the coach was doing. They were just there to keep an eye on the kids and make sure they didn't get too wild. No sniffing markers or sword-fighting with scissors. Other than that, they didn't really care what the students did. It was like a free period. And most of the adults were standing around chatting with each other casually.

Erin felt her pockets for her phone, but it wasn't there. She had left it in her purse, and had left the purse in a locked class-room with other volunteers' purses so that they wouldn't be at risk of being lost or stolen while they worked with the kids.

Erin sat on the floor, trying to catch the eye of a staff member who could unlock the classroom. She tried to keep her movements casual, hyperaware of the coach's eyes on her the whole time.

"Peter, could you do something for me?"

Peter looked at her, his face open and guileless. Always happy to help his favorite baker. She was the one who had brought the blessing of widely varying desserts and other baked goods into his life, rather than having to forever rely on commercial boxes of cookies and bags of bread. For a kid to have all of the variety that his friends could have was a huge deal. And that was why Erin did it.

"What do you want, Miss Erin?"

"I wonder if you would go over where Vice Principal Fitzroy is. Pretend you are looking for another color or marker, or that one of these ran out and you need the same color to finish your card."

He frowned at her. "Okay… why?"

"Make sure that no one else is listening or watching you, and ask Mr. Fitzroy if he would let me into the classroom to get my purse. Tell him I'm not feeling very well."

Peter nodded, looking concerned. "Are you sick?"

"I'm… well, I'm not feeling the best. You remember I had a car accident? It's been kind of hard on me if I try to do too much. I think I have done too much, and I'd better go home."

"Okay." He frowned again, obviously wondering why he had to go through the charade of looking for a marker and making sure no one was listening. Why didn't she just go over there herself and ask him?

Erin didn't fill him in. She just nodded, encouraging him to go. Peter picked up one of the markers and walked over to the table beside the vice principal, where there was a plastic bin of markers. He pawed through it, pretending to look for something. He looked at Mr. Fitzroy and looked around him to see if anyone else was watching or listening. He looked at Erin to make sure he was doing what she wanted him to. Erin nodded again, encouraging him to keep doing what she had said.

Peter saw Coach Hadrian, and Erin saw sudden understanding flood over his features. He could see the way that the coach was looking at Erin and knew that there was something wrong. Maybe he connected it up with their conversation, or maybe he hadn't made the full leap yet.

He tugged at the vice principal's sleeve to get his attention. Mr. Fitzroy looked down at him, asking a question.

Peter answered him and, after a moment, Fitzroy was looking over at Erin. He started to walk over, one hand going to his pocket to jingle his keys. Peter walked with him.

Erin pretended that she was still looking at the cards of Peter's friends and talking with them about what they were doing. She tried not to do anything that would give away to Coach Hadrian that she had figured out his game and was trying to get away so that she could take action.

Then Fitzroy stopped to talk to Hadrian. Peter's eyes got wide, and he tried to tug Mr. Fitzroy away from Hadrian, over to Erin. He flashed a look at Erin, wide-eyed, desperate.

Hadrian must have seen that look. He glanced from Peter to Erin, and a flush started to spread up his neck. She could see his mouth form the word 'no.' He must have said it out loud, because Fitzroy looked startled and confused. Fitzroy looked around.

Looking for an escape route? Looking for some of his prize athletes to help him out?

Erin remembered Hadrian's words about Joshua.

I've talked to Josh a few times to try to convince him to play.

Did Joshua know about Hadrian's side play? Did he know about Hadrian coaching his students to burglarize homes, not just to win school games? Was that why he had dropped out of sports and refused to go back?

It made sense that it was the coach. He was used to telling the boys what to do. Telling them exactly how to behave and live their lives. She didn't know what he could have said to convince them to steal people's Christmas presents, but he probably hadn't had to do a lot of convincing if he offered them each a cut. A few special video games or consoles. *What do you want for Christmas? All you have to do is what I say, and you can have it.*

He had been unconcerned about the children whose Christmas had been ruined by his plundering.

If these kids were not coddled and babied so much, they would be able to withstand more of the hard knocks.

She tried to gather herself together, pulling her legs in and getting ready to jump to her feet. She didn't know what Hadrian would do, whether he would cut and run now that he thought he was discovered, or whether he would come after her. He had run her off the road or ordered her to be run off the road once before. There was no telling what he would do if cornered.

But she couldn't run. Her purse and her phone were locked up and she had no car. She didn't want to leave with Peter standing so close to Hadrian; what if he decided to take a hostage and reached for the closest kid?

She wanted to call Peter to come over to her but was afraid that if she did so, it would just point Hadrian in her direction. That was the last thing she wanted. She tried to communicate with him with only her eyes. Peter stared at her, his eyes wide, frozen in place.

Fitzroy put his hands down on Peter's shoulders and said something to him, smiling genially. Peter turned and ran from the gym. Several people turned around to look at him, drawn by the sound of running feet amid the murmur of children coloring, cutting, and pasting. Fitzroy spoke to Hadrian for another minute, then continued toward Erin.

She let out her breath. Hadrian stayed where he was, still staring at her with malice, but not making any move to attack her or to take any of the innocent children nearby hostage. If he had any sense, he'd wait until she was out of the room and then run. He could make a clean getaway before she had a chance to report him. He just had to hold it together long enough.

Erin rose to her feet as Fitzroy got within a couple of strides of her.

"Miss Price, you're not feeling very well?" the vice principal asked with a concerned smile.

"No, I'm sorry. I thought I would be able to last the whole time, but I don't have a lot of stamina since the accident. I need to get home to where I can lie down."

He nodded his agreement and took her solicitously by the arm as if she were an old lady who needed to be helped or she might fall down. Erin let him. If he could just extract her from the gym, she would be safe. She could call Terry. She could give him a heads-up that the coach was the mastermind behind the burglaries. They would be able to track and capture Hadrian, and everything would be fine.

She was aware that she was breathing too fast. Her heart was pumping so fast she felt like it would burst right out of her chest.

"It was a shame to hear about your accident," Fitzroy said. "I was very sorry to hear what had happened."

Erin nodded. "I was fortunate. I should have been killed, or at least injured pretty badly. Who would have thought my little beater would stand up to that kind of abuse and I would walk away?"

She watched the faces of the people they passed, looking for anyone who understood what was going on and might interfere. How many boys were on the coach's teams? It had to be a good percentage of the boys in the upper grades. It wasn't that big a school.

How many were firmly enough under his control to take action to keep her from getting to a phone and informing on them? They would want to keep their coach safe from investigation. It was because of him that they could get the loot that they wanted; money, games, and whatever else they had wanted from the homes they robbed. The coach would only want liquid assets. Cash and whatever he could quickly convert at a pawn shop or fence in the city.

Some of the teens were definitely watching her with suspicion. They would have been warned about talking to her. They would have heard about the failed attempt to put her out of action. They would know that she was the girlfriend of one of the town's police officers.

She didn't remember the hallways being so long. The floors were a nondescript white pattern, buffed to a shine. The walls were covered with bulletin boards showcasing student work, posters, and seasonal topics. Very cheerful. How many different schools had she gone to that were exactly the same?

"Here we are," Fitzroy said, stopping her. He pulled out his keys and picked through them to find the right one. "Do you need someone to drive you home?"

"No. I'll be fine to walk."

"I don't like to let you do that when you're not feeling well. It wouldn't be very gentlemanly of me."

Erin swallowed. She glanced at him sideways, trying not to stare or make eye contact as she tried to figure out whether he might be involved as well. He seemed so nice, so charming, but that could be a facade.

She had dealt with enough parents and authority figures in the past who were able to put on a convincing front, but who behind closed doors were completely different people. Fitzroy gave no indication that he thought anything was wrong or out of place.

He unlocked the door and let Erin go over to the table to pick out her purse. Relieved, Erin reached to pick it up.

She thought fleetingly of what might be in the other purses there. If she went straight for her purse, was she giving up the opportunity to arm herself with pepper spray or something more lethal? She was not experienced in using pepper spray or firearms, but it seemed easy enough. Aim and press the button or pull the trigger. Vic had encouraged her more than once to protect herself by carrying a gun and learning how to use it. Erin had refused on more than one occasion, and yet she kept finding herself in circumstances where it might have been helpful to have been able to defend herself.

Except that people were killed by their own guns as often as they managed to kill or hold off their attackers. Any weapon that she used could be turned and used against her if she were not well-coordinated and experienced enough to use it properly. Whose purses were there? Who did she know carried pepper spray? At least that wouldn't kill her if someone turned it against her.

"Can't find it?" Fitzroy prompted.

"It's here somewhere." Erin moved her body in between Fitzroy, who was still standing in the doorway of the classroom and the table. She didn't want him to be able to see what she was doing or to decide to come over to help her out.

It was silly to be worrying about weapons. She had left Coach Hadrian back in the gym, and she would have Terry there in a few minutes.

But every time she had walked out of the school lately, there had been someone there waiting to talk to her. She didn't want to take the chance that the coach could have left the school and might get the drop on her.

Erin grabbed her purse. She looked at the others, but couldn't start going through them to find pepper spray. That would be too obvious. The vice principal would want to know what she was up to.

She opened her purse and felt for her phone. She wanted it in her hand. She wanted to be ready and to get Terry as soon as she could. He would help her. He'd drop everything to be there and be sure that she was safe from Hadrian and his young burglars.

"Are you all right?" Fitzroy asked as she made her way toward the door. "You're very pale. I could call the nurse. You could lie down in the first aid room until you feel better."

"No. I'm okay. Maybe… I'll just use the commode before I go."

He nodded. When she walked out of the room, he didn't leave her side. Maybe he was just careful about school security. Or maybe he was in on it with Hadrian.

Could the coach operate without any of the other adults at the school knowing what was going on? Or were there others, like Fitzroy, who looked the other direction and allowed him to get away with stealing from the people of Bald Eagle Falls? Maybe some of them were getting paid to keep quiet.

Erin let him escort her to the nearest restroom. He would have to wait outside the door.

The door closed and Erin looked around, making sure that the stalls were empty and trying to decide how to proceed. There was no way she wanted Fitzroy to be able to hear her through the door. So go into one of the stalls? Would that muffle the sound of her call enough? Or go out the second doorway at the other end of the restroom and try to get farther away from his curious ears?

Erin went to the sinks and started the water running in a couple of them, then went to the far end of the restroom and tapped her screen to call Terry.

The call went to voicemail.

Erin stared at the screen. If looks could kill, that little device would be toast. Of course, it wasn't the phone's fault if Terry rejected the call or had his phone turned to 'do not disturb.' Or maybe his phone battery had died. He was pretty good about keeping it charged, but there had been times in the past when he had been on duty for too long and hadn't had the chance to charge it and didn't have an external battery pack on him. There was already so much weight on his duty belt; the last thing he needed was another heavy piece of electronics equipment.

"Terry…" she whispered. "Come on. I need you."

She texted him an urgent message and pressed send. She watched the screen, waiting for a text back or an incoming call. She tapped her fingernail against the back of the phone, impatient. Every second seemed like an eternity. How long would it be before Fitzroy decided that there was something wrong and came into the bathroom after her? She glanced toward the door. If only he would just stay out there, or get distracted by something else, she could find someone who could help her.

The police dispatcher was the next most logical call. It didn't matter which of the police officers came to her aid, as long as someone did. Someone experienced who could protect her from Hadrian.

But one man against Hadrian was not enough. What if he

called on his chosen athletes to help him? How many were there? Was it just a handful of them? A few carefully-selected individuals who he knew would be loyal to him and do whatever he asked? Or was it most of the boys on his teams? Most of the boys in the upper grades? Whoever came to her rescue might have to face multiple attackers. And who would want to fight a kid? Their first reaction would be to protect the children, not to see them as a threat.

She tried the police dispatch number. Hopefully, everyone wasn't off chatting as they finished organizing the Christmas packages. Someone would still be manning the phones. Crime didn't stop just because there were Christmas hampers to be organized.

It rang a few times, and Erin was swearing in her head, biting her lip, and keeping an eye on the door.

"Come on, come on," she murmured urgently.

Finally, a familiar voice answered the phone. "Bald Eagle Falls, emergency dispatch."

CHAPTER 34

*E*rin breathed a sigh of relief.

"It's Erin Price. I'm at the school. I need… help. Is Terry available? He didn't answer his phone."

"Officer Piper is not on call right now; I'm not sure where he might be. What's wrong, Miss Price? Are you in danger?"

"I think… I think I know who the head of the burglary ring is, and he's here. I think he knows I figured it out…"

"Where are you now? Are you safe?"

"I'm hiding in a restroom."

"So he isn't there right now. Does he know where you are?"

"No… but I don't know who else knows and might be in on it. Fitzroy knows where I am. Other people probably saw me come in here. Some of the other students… who knows how many of them are involved, or which ones of them are…"

"Are there any weapons? Are you in immediate danger?"

"No. Not immediate."

"And who is it you're afraid of? Who do you think is heading up the burglary ring?"

"Coach Hadrian."

There was a sharp intake of breath. One brief break in the

dispatcher's professionalism, then her businesslike voice was back. "Okay. And Coach Hadrian is at the school right now? Where and when did you see him last?"

"He was in the gym about five minutes ago. Maybe less. But I think he's onto me, so he might bolt. Can you send someone?"

"I already have a unit on its way. I'm going to direct him to the gym first, if you're safe where you are for the moment."

"Yes, okay." Erin gulped. She wished that it was Terry. She wished she knew that he was on his way to get her and that he would come directly to her. "The gym is full of children."

"Thanks for letting me know that. Do you know if he is armed? Have you seen any weapons?"

"No, I haven't seen any."

"Has he made any threats?"

"No. He didn't say anything to me. He just… looked at me. In a threatening way."

"Units are arriving at the school now. You won't hear them; they are not using sirens. Just stay where you are."

Erin was quiet, straining her ears to hear what was going on, even though the dispatcher had said they would be arriving without sirens. She listened for screams, gunshots, heavy police shoes on the run.

But everything seemed quiet.

"Are you still there, Miss Price?"

Erin nodded and swallowed. She licked her lips, wishing her mouth wasn't so dry. She was in the bathroom with the water running but hadn't thought to take a drink. "Yes. I'm here."

"What restroom are you in?"

"I don't really know my way around the school. Close to the kindergarten rooms, I think. Mr. Fitzroy was standing outside the door, but I don't know if he still is."

"Okay, someone will be there in a moment."

The door opened and, even though Erin was braced for it, she still nearly jumped out of her skin. It was Sheriff Wilmot. He looked around the room, taking in Erin and the running water in the sinks. His weapon was still in its holster, so there must not have been any violence in response to their arrival.

"Miss Price. All okay?"

She let out her breath, trying to relax. "Yeah, I'm okay. Did you find him? Coach Hadrian? Was he still there?"

The sheriff's lips pressed together in a thin line. "No, he wasn't in the gym. We'll have to find out whether anyone saw him leave. Do you want to come out of here, and we can have a chat?"

Erin nodded. She walked over to one of the taps and turned it off. Wilmot turned off the other.

"I didn't want Fitzroy to overhear my call," Erin explained. "I don't know… whether he's involved or not. He and Coach Hadrian seem pretty close. He didn't do anything, but some of the things he said… I was just worried that he might be in on it. Even if he wasn't taking part, he could know about it and be taking a cut to stay quiet." She shook her head. "I just don't know."

He led her out of the bathroom into the hallway. Fitzroy was standing a short distance away, looking confused, talking to Tom Baker. The sheriff led her away without any comment. They found an empty classroom and she and Wilmot sat down at a table and Erin explained what Peter had said and the conclusions she had come to. On repeating it, she realized that the connection was pretty tenuous and she had no real proof that Hadrian was involved, but she was still confident that it was true. It made perfect sense.

"We had come to the conclusion that there had to be at least one adult involved," the sheriff agreed. "We've talked to a number of people, but no one pointed to the coach. We didn't have anything to indicate he wasn't telling the truth. I imagine he's gone to lengths to make sure that he has alibis for the actual burglaries. Leave the kids to do the dirty work, and convince them that turning on him or the team would be a betrayal of the school and the town."

Erin nodded. "But we'll need evidence, won't we? You can't search his house for any of the stolen property until you have some real evidence that he was the one leading the burglary ring, or at least knew of it."

"Leave that to me. You don't need to be doing the investigating here."

"I know… I was just talking to Peter. I wasn't investigating."

"Make sure you keep it that way. We'll talk to Peter and to the boys on the teams to see if we can crack them."

"Peter is so young. I would never have thought that someone his age would have known anything about it."

"We certainly didn't interview anyone his age. But I supposed if it's become part of the culture of the school… then even kids as young as him are going to be conditioned to think it's okay for the elite to break the law and that it would be wrong to report them." Sheriff Wilmot didn't seem surprised that the boys on the teams had something to do with the burglaries.

"How long have you known? That the kids were involved?"

"Well… it was obvious when you were talking to the boys that something was going on at the school. The only reason they would know the things they did was if other schoolkids were involved. There was just too much awareness, even if no one knew—or admitted to knowing—exactly who was involved."

"What would make someone do something like that? How would you even think of it?" Erin shook her head. "Was he just sitting grading papers one day or yelling at a football player to complete a certain play, and thought 'why don't I start stealing from families in town?'"

"In my experience, he's probably in debt. Maybe he took up gambling. Suddenly he has a whole lot of money that he has to pay back and needs to come up with it fast. So he's willing to take a risk if there's the chance of a big payoff."

"Erin nodded slowly. "Yeah, I guess so. It just seems so… bizarre. I can't imagine anyone deciding to rip people off like that."

"That's because you're a good, decent person who tries to do what's right. Not everyone has been raised that way. Or has decided to live their lives that way."

Erin felt her face flush. She shrugged in embarrassment.

"We would hope that people who we entrust the care of our children to would have high moral standards," Wilmot said, "but that isn't always the case."

"No." Erin had direct experience with that fact.

She wondered fleetingly if she would ever have children of her own. She enjoyed being around kids, especially a friendly little fellow like Peter, but she wasn't sure if she were cut out to be a mother. Owning pets and worrying about keeping them safe and well was challenging enough.

She rubbed her forehead, trying to ease the headache that was settling in. "Do you know where Terry is?"

He shook his head. "He's not on shift. I'm not sure what his plans were. You would have a better idea than I would."

"I thought he would be helping with the Christmas hampers. But I guess you'd know if he was doing that."

"Not as far as I know. It's possible Clara sent him out to pick up something extra. He's not at your place? Having a nap, maybe?"

"I haven't been home. He didn't answer his phone."

"Might have just been asleep. He's had a lot to do the last few days."

Erin nodded. "I guess… I'll head home and find out."

"You're not in the best shape yourself. Can I drive you home?"

"You must have a lot to do here. You're still looking for Coach Hadrian?"

"I can take a few minutes out. I'd rather know that you were safely home."

"Well… okay." Erin hadn't been looking forward to walking home. While she hadn't thought about her aches and pains while the adrenaline had been coursing through her veins, it was wearing off, and she was feeling tired, sore, and shaky. It would be one thing if she had her own car to drive home. She could have managed that. But walking was a bit much.

CHAPTER 35

They didn't have much conversation on the way home. Erin rested her head against the window, eyes closed, just wanting to be home in bed. With Terry. It didn't matter that it was still early afternoon, that was what she wanted.

Sheriff Wilmot pulled up in front of the house and looked at it. "You'll be okay? Do you want to see if Officer Piper is here before you decide?"

If Terry was back at his own house, it meant that he wanted to be alone. Erin wouldn't go over without an invitation. If he needed his space, she would give it to him.

"No, it's okay."

"Do you want me to clear the house first? I highly doubt that Hadrian would come over here instead of running, but you never know."

Erin looked at the house. "The burglar alarm hasn't gone off."

"Are you sure you armed it?"

"I always set it." She thought about it, trying to recall each moment that morning before she left. She couldn't specifically remember arming the burglar alarm. She always did, but that didn't mean she had. She wasn't feeling well, and if she had been too tired or distracted, it was possible that she had missed that step in her usual routine. "Um, yeah, actually. I'll take you up on that. Just to be sure."

He nodded his agreement and opened his door. "Your key?"

Erin rifled her purse to find her ring of keys and handed it to him.

"And the passcode for the alarm?"

Erin gave it to him.

"Okay. I'll be just a minute; then you can lie down and relax."

She watched him walk up the sidewalk to the door, unlock the door, and go in. She pictured him clearing the burglar alarm, calling out to Terry to alert him if he was home, walking through the house with one hand on his gun to make sure that everything was in order and no intruders were hiding in closets or under the bed. She felt a little like a child demanding that the adult in charge check for monsters before she could go to bed.

Hadrian wouldn't have gone to her house. He would be far away.

But he had tried to run her off the road. He or one of his students. They had been willing to take that step. She remembered the vice principal's words.

I was very sorry to hear what had happened.

Sorry that she had been run off the road or sorry that she had survived? She wished that she had the answers as to who had been involved in or known about the burglaries. It was going to be a long time before she felt safe trusting anyone connected with the school.

There was a tap on her window that made Erin startle.

But it was just the sheriff. She opened the car door.

"All clear," he pronounced, handing her key ring back.

"Thank you so much. I feel like such a coward. I can't even walk into my own house by myself."

"With your record? You're not being a coward. You're being very brave. Now you take care of yourself. I'm hoping you're a lot more bright-eyed the next time I see you."

"I will be," Erin promised.

She couldn't be much worse. She was ready to pass out.

She didn't even remember walking up the sidewalk into the house.

It had been early afternoon when Erin had returned home, but it was dark when she woke up. She didn't remember everything immediately, feeling warm and comfortable and swaddled with sleepiness.

Terry was there, stroking her hair, waiting for her to wake up. "Hey, sweetie. You don't have to wake up if you don't want to, I just want to let you know I'm here."

She raised one heavy arm to touch his hand and clasp it briefly.

"You can go back to sleep," he told her

"No," Erin murmured. "I want to talk. Just give me a few minutes to wake up."

"Okay." He pushed a wisp of hair away from her eyes. "I hear that you've been cracking cases again."

"Mmm. I tried to call you."

"Sorry, I missed it. I was having a nap."

"Mmm." Erin accepted his explanation, but her brain continued to worry at the explanation. He hadn't been sleeping there. Where had he been? His own house?

And she remembered how quickly the call had gone to voicemail.

He'd rejected the call, or been in 'do not disturb' mode, or maybe his phone had been out of juice. But he hadn't just slept through it ringing for several minutes.

"A couple of the boys knew that Coach Hadrian has a fishing shack by the lake," Terry said.

For a long time, Erin just lay there, waiting for her brain to come out of sleep mode, wondering why that was important.

"Wh-what? What did you say?"

"Coach Hadrian has a fishing shack. A little bit bigger than you might think when someone uses the word 'shack.'"

"Did you catch him?"

"Can't say *I* had much to do with it. Stayner was the one who headed out there while I was napping the afternoon away."

"Me too."

"Yeah. A great pair."

"I was so tired." Erin rubbed her eyes. "So Stayner got him? He's in custody? But there's no proof that he was the one leading the burglary ring…"

"Did I mention that he had a lot of loot stashed at the fishing shack? That's why he went straight there when he figured you were onto him."

"Oh, good." Erin pushed herself up a little and readjusted her pillow. If she could get closer to sitting up, she'd be able to chase the cobwebs away more quickly. "And… no one got hurt?"

"Stayner shouldn't have gone in by himself, but he was okay. No gunfire. And he found a truck parked by the shack. In addition to the one Hadrian had driven out there."

"Mmm-hm."

"Do you want me to turn on the lamp?"

"Yes."

Terry fumbled for a moment and then turned it on. Erin blinked painfully in the flood of light.

"You found a truck?" she repeated.

"Yes."

"Was it the one he hit me with?"

"Looks that way. We'll have to test the paint, but it has a dented front end. I'm pretty sure it was the truck that rammed you."

Erin took a deep breath and let it out slowly. "So you got him. You've really got him, there's no question."

"I would say so. We've got him all wrapped up in a neat little package." Terry chuckled. "A very special Christmas present just for you."

"Best Christmas present ever. It's such a relief."

"I thought it would be."

"Do they know if there was anyone else involved? Or anyone else who knew about it and didn't tell? Besides the kids, I mean."

"That is going to take somewhat longer to figure out. I'm hoping that we'll be able to sort that out as we interview the teens who were involved."

"Do you think you'll be able to identify all of the kids who were working for him? And are they guilty, or were they coerced?" Erin sat up the rest of the way, awake and her brain working now.

"That will have to be decided on an individual basis. I imagine we'll have the whole range, from kids who were eager to get involved and suggesting the houses to hit to those who were forced to participate or pass on information."

"They knew which families to hit because they had a pretty good idea what the other kids were supposed to be getting and what their families' schedules were."

"Yeah."

"Did some of them hit their own families?"

"Undoubtedly. And they would get double the loot because they get what they stole and then what the town fundraised to give them a second present." He shook his head in disgust. "Some people have no scruples."

"Yeah."

"And the community center? Turns out that the woman who keeps the keys has a son on the basketball team."

"And he took it to break in and get the needy children's toys."

Terry nodded, rubbing the back of his head. "Like I said… no scruples."

Erin stretched her limbs, seeing how her body felt. "Do you want anything to eat?"

"I can get something out. Are you hungry?"

"Just sort of peckish. But I know I should eat."

"Come on out, then. You can sit while I make you something."

"I can make dinner."

"No, you can't. You can sit at the table and watch me."

Erin laughed and shook her head. "Okay, fine. I'll sit and watch."

CHAPTER 36

The day before Christmas had been busy as they made sure that the rest of the Christmas packages were delivered so that children would be able to wake up with presents under the tree. Erin was tired, but not exhausted as she had been previously. She was glad to know that everybody would be getting a day off. She wouldn't be missing her shift at Auntie Clem's Bakery and making someone else cover for her; they would all be off and able to enjoy time with their families. And after that, she thought, she'd be able to get back to a regular schedule.

It surprised her how hard it was to be limited by her physical health. She usually had the stamina she needed to get up early and work through the day. It was a big change to only be able to stand for a few minutes or an hour at a time. It gave her more sympathy for Terry, who'd been struggling with his body's limitations since the attack. She'd understood that it was difficult, but not how frustrating it was to be battling against her own body.

Christmas Eve arrived and Erin sat on the couch cuddled up to Terry with the animals all in a happy, relaxed state. Erin picked up Orange Blossom and cuddled him, happy that he was well and back to normal after their scare.

"This is nice," she told Terry. "Just how I wanted it to be."

"But this is pretty much the same as every other night."

"Yes."

He laughed. "Well, Christmas Eve is our time. Then tomorrow… you'll have to deal with company."

"It will be nice to have everyone together again." Erin shook her head. "It's been strange with everyone going in different directions. I feel like we haven't seen anyone."

He nodded.

It had been uncomfortable being at odds with Terry, too. She wasn't used to arguing with him. Not seriously. "Is this okay? Us just being with each other for Christmas Eve?"

"Sure."

"You don't want to… go to Christmas services tonight? There's a candlelight service at First Baptist."

"How do you know that?"

"I hear things."

He considered the question for a minute. "I'm okay just being home with you. I don't feel the need to go to church."

"But would you rather go than not go? If you weren't with me, would you go?"

"I don't know."

"What have you done the last few years, before you met me?"

Terry scratched his ear. "You're quite the interrogator. Other years, I have usually gone to Christmas Eve services."

"You could go this year."

"I know. But I'll stay with you."

"What if I said I'd go? Would you go then?"

Terry raised one eyebrow and studied her face. "It really isn't that big of a deal. I believe what I believe, whether I go to services or not."

"I'll go."

"You said *this* is just what you wanted."

"That doesn't mean we can't do what you want too. It would only be, what, an hour out of our evening?"

Terry nodded.

"Then why don't we go?"

The church was already quiet when Erin arrived with Terry, people speaking in whispers as they distributed candles and herded their families into the chapel. But when they saw Erin, everyone froze. The whispers stopped and for a moment, there was complete silence. Then Melissa jumped forward.

"Erin, isn't this nice! I wasn't expecting you to join us today. Each of you grab a candle," she passed a tall white candle to Erin. "I really do think this is the most beautiful service of the year. Then find a seat in the chapel. There are no reserved spots; you can sit anywhere."

"Thank you."

"I'd suggest a few rows from the front. You want to be able to see the children."

"Okay, thanks."

Melissa patted Terry on the arm and left them to their own devices.

"You still okay with this?" Terry asked, looking down at Erin.

"Yes. It all looks very nice."

Even so, she did feel awkward and uncertain as people around her whispered and eyed her. She had hoped that people would be too excited about Christmas to take notice of her appearance, but she had underestimated people's level of interest in what she did.

The chapel was quieter than the lobby, with just the rustle of clothing as the worshipers found their seats. Terry led her up the aisle to a bench close to the front.

"How is this?"

Erin nodded silently. They shuffled down the bench to the end and sat down. Erin tried to look around and see everything she could without swiveling her head back and forth like a tourist. It was a pretty little church, with some stained glass windows and ornamental carvings. Not too dark. She was glad to see that the cross at the front of the chapel did not display the tortured Christ, but was simple and unadorned. As a child, she'd been horrified and fascinated by the cruel crucifixes displayed in churches she'd been dragged to.

Terry took her hand in his and gave it a little squeeze. He didn't whisper to her anymore, not wanting to disturb the stillness of the place, but he kissed the corner of her forehead, and she knew he was thanking her for joining him for the service.

Erin watched the congregants make their way to their seats, focusing on the families with teens and young children. Most of them were smiling as they looked around and waited for the candlelight service to begin. Maybe they still would have been happy even if they hadn't gotten any Christmas presents, but Erin was glad that they hadn't had to find out.

CHAPTER 37

*E*rin and Vic were up early to get the turkey stuffed and cooking and to put a couple of trays of cinnamon buns in the second oven to start the day properly with a sugar-induced haze. They were joined before long by Adele, who smiled uncertainly at Vic and offered to help with whatever she could. It was a bit crowded for the three of them to work in the kitchen, but Erin made space the best she could and included Adele.

"So, what's this I hear about you going to the First Baptist service last night?" Adele inquired.

"I didn't," Vic said with a frown, turning to look at her. "I know they won't accept me like this, and I'm not going to hide who I am for a church service. Willie and I went into the city; there was an LGBT-friendly service at one of the missions downtown."

Adele quirked an eyebrow and shook her head. "No. Not you. Erin."

"Erin?" Vic put down her spatula and looked at Erin. "*You* went to First Baptist?"

Erin swallowed and stared down at the buns she was icing. She wasn't sure how Adele managed to hear everything that went on in town. She hardly associated with anyone, yet she always seemed to know what was going on.

"Uh, yes. I went with Terry to the candlelight service."

"How did he talk you into that? I'm going to have to have a word with him!"

"He didn't coerce me. He was happy just to stay home together, but I didn't want him to miss out on it because of me. So I offered to go with him."

"That was so nice of you. And so… what did you think?"

"It was nicely done. Very peaceful and pleasant. Lots of families there, so they kept it short. Kind of a nice way to start off the holiday."

"And did you feel…" Vic hesitated and shook her head, trying to put it into words. "Did you feel like it was…"

"I wasn't converted," Erin said, her face getting hot, "if that's what you're wondering. I'm not planning to start going to church services every week. It was just something that I did with Terry. Because of his beliefs, not mine."

"Yeah, okay. I just wasn't sure how it would make you feel. Whether…" Vic was getting a little pink herself. "Whether it would *move* you."

"I'm still the same Erin. Still an atheist."

Vic shrugged. "Okay, just asking. It was nice of you to go."

Erin continued to ice the buns. "And your service in the city? Was it good? You enjoyed it?"

"Yes, it was really friendly. I felt like I belonged there, instead of being an outsider. I like Bald Eagle Falls, but I know what would happen if I attended church here. It would not be fun."

"And Willie? Did he like it? I don't even know if he's Christian or not. I guess he is…?"

"I'd say he probably identifies as Christian, but not as any particular sect, and he doesn't see the need to go to church to worship. He's not against it; he just doesn't see the point when he has so many other things he wants to do. Last night was something special, like with you and Terry. Something that he tagged along for because he figured it would make me happy."

"And did it?"

Vic's eyes cut over to Erin. "I didn't drag him along. I wouldn't do it if I thought he didn't want to. So… yes, it made me happy that he could be there with me too. I didn't want to go by myself, and leave him all alone Christmas Eve."

They went on with the breakfast and dinner preparations, listening to Terry watching *A Christmas Carol*. Willie wasn't there yet. Jeremy and Beaver were supposed to be joining them.

"It's nice to have a place where we can all gather around the table and be welcome, no matter what our beliefs," Adele murmured.

"Yes, it is," Erin agreed. In the Bible belt, where everyone was expected to be Christian at least in name, it was difficult sometimes to make people understand that being an atheist—or a witch—didn't mean you were an evil person, just that you had different beliefs. It was nice to have a port in a storm, people who were close to her who didn't care whether they shared religious beliefs or not, who liked her for who she was.

Erin was sitting back in her chair, belly fully, contemplating whether she dared have just one more Grinch cookie or whether it would make her stomach hurt for the rest of the day, when the doorbell rang.

"Carolers?" Jeremy asked. "You weren't expecting anyone, were you?"

"No, I wasn't expecting anyone else today." Erin pushed herself up off of her chair and decided it was probably a good idea if she didn't try to fit one more cookie into her full stomach. She made her way to the door and opened it without checking the peephole first. There were plenty of people there to protect her. Who was going to cause trouble on Christmas day? Everyone would be spending time with their own families. Although—Erin had a chill as she opened the door that wasn't from the weather—they still hadn't managed to track down crazy Theresa. And they couldn't be sure that they had identified everyone who had been involved in the burglary ring. Maybe she ought to be more cautious about opening the door without checking first.

It was Joshua. No weapon, of course, not standing there with lasers shooting out his eyes, as Mary Lou's would surely do if she knew he was there. Joshua stood there awkwardly, one foot behind him with the toe digging into the step as if he were trying to drill a hole with it.

"Merry Christmas, Miss Erin."

"Hi, Joshua. It's nice to see you. How is everything?"

Joshua looked past Erin and saw all of the people seated around the table. "Oh, I didn't mean to disturb you. You're in the middle of dinner."

"No, we're done. Do you want to come in? There are still more cookies…"

He shook his head, looking away from her. "I just… I wanted to apologize for my mom. I don't know why she went off on you like that. I mean, she knows how you tried to help us out before, and you were there after Campbell was arrested and you never shunned her like other folks did for what Dad did. And he even tried to kill you."

Erin didn't say 'twice.' That might have been pushing it when he was in mid-apology.

"You don't need to apologize for Mary Lou. I know she was just trying to protect you, and she was afraid I was going to get you in trouble when you hadn't done anything. She's afraid, after what happened to Campbell, that the same thing could happen to you."

"I know… but it was still wrong for her to get after you. You didn't do anything. The cops would have come to talk to me anyway."

"Maybe," Erin agreed. "But as it was, they did come after you because of what I'd said. I never thought you were committing the burglaries, but I was confused about what Ha—about what one of the boys said to me. I didn't think that you would be involved in anything like that."

"I could have been," Joshua pointed out. He cleared his throat. "A lot of the boys were."

Erin stepped out of the house and pointed down at the steps. She and Joshua sat down together to talk. "A lot of the boys were," she agreed. "It's really hard to believe that the coach could talk them into it. Could brainwash them like that so that no one would even report it."

"He really wanted me to join up again. To be on all of his teams. I think maybe he thought that if I did, Campbell would decide to come back. I don't know. It's stupid. But I don't think he really wanted me. It wasn't like I was an all-star. He just thought that if he could get one of the Cox boys, he could get both of us. And Cam was a lot better than me."

"It must have been so hard for you when Campbell left."

"I wish he hadn't gone away. But I know… he couldn't stay. He couldn't keep going on like he was, or it would have killed him. He couldn't take the stress and the expectations."

"You boys have had to go through so much. And I know that you're still struggling. I didn't mean to cause you any extra stress because of what I said. You didn't need being accused and interrogated by the police on top of everything else."

Joshua pulled up the hood on his hoodie and cuddled up in it, arms wrapped around himself. "It was actually kind of cool," he said with a wicked grin. "You see this stuff on TV all the time, and you wonder how much is real and how much is just made up for drama. And to actually be caught in the middle of a thing like this…"

"You enjoyed it?" Erin said in disbelief.

"I don't know if 'enjoyed' is the right word, but it was interesting. I was anxious, but I didn't really think they were going to put me in jail or that anyone was going to set me up like they did

Campbell. So I wasn't really worried that they were somehow going to find some evidence that pointed to me."

"I'm glad."

"Maybe I'll write it all down and make a script or screenplay sometime. My own cop show."

"I didn't know you were interested in writing."

"Well… I don't tell a lot of people. Because of Campbell, they expect me to be a jock and to get honors in everything. And I don't sit around writing in my spare time. It's just… something I'd like to do some time."

"Did you write down what happened when we were looking for Brianna?"

He took a covert look around and then nodded. "In a notebook. I write little things in there sometimes. Just… thoughts… ideas… things maybe I'd like to write about someday. It's not a journal. Just… a notebook."

They sat on the steps in silence for a while. Erin shifted, her tailbone starting to ache from the cold concrete. "Did you know what was going on with Coach Hadrian and the team? Did you know that they were the ones who were committing the robberies and that he was at the head of it?"

Joshua pursed his lips and considered. "No, not really… but there was talk about there being secrets and that the coach was doing something… I was worried at first that he was molesting them or something, but when I talked to Campbell, he said there was never anything like that. The coach didn't ever touch them or hang out in the locker room. Of course, then he wanted to know why I was asking…" Joshua rolled his eyes. "Talk about drama. So I just put it out of my mind. Figured maybe they were throwing games for him. I didn't know that they had anything to do with the burglaries. But I don't hang out with anyone on the teams anymore. When I dropped out of them… the other players pretty much shunned me. No one wanted anything to do with me. And I guess it was a lucky thing that they didn't."

"I'm very glad that you weren't involved."

"That's just not the kind of guy I am." Joshua contemplated a hole worn in his jeans. "You know… I'd rather give up my own presents and see little kids happy at Christmas. I'd never steal from them. I know what it's like to struggle now, like I never did before Dad lost everything… and I'd rather have nothing than put someone else through that."

Erin put her arm around his shoulders and hugged him. "You're a special guy, Joshua."

"Special," Joshua echoed in a mocking tone.

"I don't mean it in a mean way. Really. I like you, and I like the kind of guy you are. You're going to be a great catch for a girl someday."

He chuckled. "Thanks. I wonder sometimes. I don't exactly see myself as the type of knight in shining armor that girls want to sweep them off of their feet."

"You don't need to be a knight. And you don't have to be flashy. One day, they'll recognize what a good guy you are, and you'll have the kind of girl who will support and encourage you."

Joshua nodded, swallowing a few times, and couldn't seem to get any other words out. Erin turned her face away from his to give him a chance to collect himself.

"I'd better get back in there. Don't worry about your mom. I know she was under a lot of stress and she's just worried about you. We'll work it out. Do you want some treats to take home?"

"Well… I probably shouldn't."

"Why not? Do you have any idea how many desserts we end up throwing out around here? We've always got too much to eat ourselves. I'll make you a plate."

"That might kind of give away where I've been."

"You don't want Mary Lou to know that you came here?"

He shook his head.

"Well, just a couple of cookies then. One for each hand."

Joshua grinned. "Well, if you're that set on getting rid of them."

"I am."

"Okay."

Erin returned to the house while he waited on the steps.

"Everything okay?" Terry asked.

"Yes, just fine."

"He's not bothering you?"

"No. He was apologizing. And talking about what happened. I'm just going to get a couple of cookies for him."

She felt like all eyes were on her as she looked over the dessert platter and grabbed two cookies for Josh. She glanced around at her guests, and they mostly looked away. Beaver continued to look at her.

"Do you think I should talk to him too?" Beaver asked.

"Mary Lou was pretty clear that she wanted you to stay away from him, so I wouldn't if I were you. Just stay clear until things have settled down again. Even then… I don't know. She doesn't want him involved in any of your investigations."

Beaver popped a couple of sticks of gum in her mouth. "Too bad. He's very observant. And more discreet than his brother. I wouldn't mind having his insight."

Erin shook her head and took the cookies out to Joshua.

CHAPTER 38

Everyone had made their way back to their own homes. Erin and Terry had both had a nap in the afternoon. With how exhausted Erin had been since the accident, she wasn't worried that having a rest would ruin her sleep for that night.

A couple of hours later, they were both up again spending some quiet time cuddling and watching whatever Christmas movies were still on the TV.

Terry muted it and turned to Erin during a commercial. "I have something for you."

Erin looked at him, shaking her head slightly. "What?"

He snaked his hand down into his pocket and drew out a velvet box with the name of a jeweler stamped on it in gold. Erin looked at it, her heart pounding.

"A Christmas present?" she asked. "I didn't get you anything."

"Yes, you did. You gave me your time, a great dinner with friends, and you went to the candlelight service with me, just because you wanted me to have a good Christmas. It doesn't have to be wrapped up with a bow to be a Christmas present." He looked at the little box. "I didn't even wrap this one up with a bow."

Erin shook her head. She took the box from his hand hesitantly, wondering what it was going to be and what she would say to him. She wasn't sure it was time to be getting engaged, or if she ever wanted to get married. Their argument had made her reevaluate their relationship and, even though she fully intended to stay with him, she couldn't say that it would be forever, or that they would ever get married. If his plans were different from hers…

"It's okay," Terry said, stroking the hair beside her face and following one tendril down to her neck. "Trust me."

Erin took a deep breath and opened the box.

It was not an engagement ring, but a locket. Erin examined it, smiling. "It's beautiful, Terry." It had her initials engraved on it. No message from him and not his initials, only hers.

She ran her thumbnail around the crack between the halves of the locket and pried it open. There was no picture inside, just a flat, smooth glassy surface.

"It's electronic," Terry said. "Like one of those picture frames. It loads and charges wirelessly. You can put as many pictures in it as you like."

Erin beamed.

"You tend to collect people, and I couldn't imagine you picking just one or two people to put in it," Terry went on. "This way, you can include everyone you love."

She should have trusted him. He really did know her.

Terry reached over and clicked the top of the locket. It lit up and, as Erin watched, she saw pictures of Terry, Vic, Charley, and even her dead parents, Clementine, and Bertie Braceling. She teared up.

"It's perfect, Terry. Thank you so much."

"Merry Christmas, Erin. And may the next year bring everything you want."

"And nothing that you don't," Erin finished.

He looked at her and shook his head, eyes twinkling.

Neither of them knew what the New Year would bring, but it seemed like things were never quiet for long in Bald Eagle Falls.

Did you enjoy this book? Reviews and recommendations are vital to making a book successful.

Please leave a review at your favorite book store or review site and share it with your friends.

Don't miss the following bonus material:
Sign up for mailing list to get a free ebook
Read a sneak preview chapter
Other books by P.D. Workman
Learn more about the author

Sign up for my mailing list at pdworkman.com and get Gluten-Free Murder for free!

JOIN MY MAILING LIST AND

Download a sweet mystery for free

PREVIEW OF COLD AS ICE CREAM

As soon as Erin got home from work, Orange Blossom was underfoot, meowing and yowling in greeting, winding around her legs, telling her all about his busy (or not so busy) day at home. Erin put down her purse and took off her jacket and picked him up.

"Hey. Quiet down. Relax. This is the time I get home every day, I'm not late."

He started purring, a loud rumble that filled the room. Erin pressed her face into the short velvety hair at the top of his head and scratched under his chin.

"There. You like that, huh?"

Marshmallow hopped out from behind the couch and nuzzled Erin's toes while waiting patiently for Erin to scratch his long ears.

Terry looked out from the kitchen. His jaw was dark with five o'clock shadow. He'd had an early shift and clearly hadn't shaved afterward.

"Whatever he is telling you about me, it isn't true."

Erin stroked Blossom's back, smoothing down his ruffled fur. "I think he's telling me about K9."

"You'd think he would be used to K9. Most other cats would have resigned themselves to a dog being around here by now."

Erin nodded. She could see K9 lying on the kitchen floor behind Terry, bored or tired after his patrol with Terry. Terry still wasn't back to working full-time at the police department since he had been attacked during an investigation. He was getting gradually better, but was still suffering from headaches, insomnia, and problems with concentration. Not something you wanted to worry about with your police force. K9 had been his partner for a long time and was used to patrolling all day.

"Maybe it's because K9 chased him when he was a kitten," Erin said, "back when we first met. K9 really scared Blossom, so maybe he was traumatized... instead of it being like a normal situation."

Terry raised an eyebrow. "I'd forgotten all about that," he said. "Funny. That seems like a long time ago."

"Maybe she has some kitty PTSD," Erin said, cuddling Orange Blossom up to her face again. "And here we are, just trying to get him to be friends with the person—animal—who traumatized him."

Terry rolled his eyes. "Well, something to think about. Are you hungry?" He segued to food, which Erin assumed was to avoid discussing PTSD any further. Neither of them was particularly good at discussing their feelings or their own symptoms. Terry had been mandated to undergo some counseling through the police department following his attack; he probably wouldn't have chosen to do it himself. Erin had been to enough headshrinkers in the past that she really didn't want to have to deal with another. She would do the best she could to deal with the nightmares and other issues that she had. At least after going through his own ordeal, Terry had stopped suggesting she get therapy. It seemed like a pat, easy answer, but it wasn't as simple as it sounded. It wasn't a matter of going to see a doctor, getting a prescription, and being okay. Even with intense, ongoing therapy, it could last for years and, while pills could help with the depression and some of the symptoms, they didn't fix the underlying problem with the brain.

"Yes. I don't know what you made, but it smells wonderful." Erin put Orange Blossom down and entered the kitchen. Marshmallow hopped along beside her, still waiting for attention. Erin looked at the red sauce bubbling in the pot and the various other pots and bowls on the stove and counter and smiled. "Wow, you went all out. This looks great." She bent down and petted Marshmallow. Terry wasn't an experienced cook, so she wasn't sure how any of the dishes had turned out, but he had obviously been pretty busy since he'd gotten off of his shift.

"I wanted to buckle down and make you a real meal for once. Not just a sandwich or warming up a can of soup. I keep promising to make you something, so…" He gestured along the length of the cluttered counters. "There you go. That's what I did. If you don't like it… well…"

"You must have been talking to Vic and Willie," Erin suggested. She remembered Vic getting after Willie and telling him that opening a can of soup did not constitute making her dinner. Not for a date night, anyway. Maybe other nights of the week it would be acceptable.

"Well, to Willie," Terry admitted. "We're going to do another fishing trip soon. He says it's a good time of year for…" Terry trailed off. "Hmm. I don't remember. But something is good this time of year. I don't think it really matters, as long as we have something to do while we sit around and relax. So no one calls us lazy. If you fish all day, then even if you don't come home with food, people still think that you've spent your day being productive. Not quite the same as if you just sit on the couch all day."

Erin nodded. She went to the cupboard to get out the dishes they would need. She cleared various items off of the table, which he had apparently used as a preparation area when he ran out of counter space, and set out the plates and cups. She cleared various open containers of ingredients as Terry started to fill serving dishes and take them to the table. That way, when they were done, there wouldn't be so much to clean up. Erin always felt more tired after she'd had a chance to sit down and eat. Best to get it done before the lethargy overtook her.

There were some odds and ends of vegetables left over from Terry making a salad, and she fed a few pieces to Marshmallow. Orange Blossom started to yowl and complain about how she was feeding Marshmallow and hadn't yet given him a treat.

"Okay, okay. Your treat is coming." Erin let herself into the pantry, but pushed him back and wouldn't allow him to follow her in there. A few weeks ago, she wouldn't have bothered, but since he had gotten sick, apparently after having eaten something he shouldn't have, she was far more careful about keeping him away from people food, whether it was something she thought would be okay for cats or not. He was only allowed to eat food that came in a package with a picture of a cat on the side.

And the crumbs that K9 left behind. Once Erin had slid a few treats across the floor for Orange Blossom to chase, she got a gluten-free doggie biscuit out of the cookie jar and gave it to K9. He lay with it between his paws, munching on it. Blossom saw that his adversary had also been given a treat and, after gobbling down his own, he slunk closer to K9 to see if he could snatch a few crumbs. It was the only time he would get close to the shepherd without hissing and puffing his fur out.

With the food preparation areas mostly cleared, Erin sat down to eat with Terry, looking over the variety of dishes that he had put together.

"This looks great," she told him.

Terry beamed.

CHAPTER 2

She was happy that Terry was feeling well enough after an early shift to cook a meal for her. A few weeks before, that wouldn't have been possible. He had barely been able to get through his half-shifts, let alone do anything productive afterward.

They sat on the couch after eating, sharing details about their days.

Nothing exciting had happened, and that was perfectly fine. They didn't need any more crime or mysteries. Just routine, everyday baking and policing work. Muffins and parking tickets.

There was a knock at the back door, then the sound of the door opening and Vic's voice. "Y'all decent?"

Erin straightened slightly and smiled at her young employee. "What would you do if we weren't?"

"Well, I guess I'd go all the way back to the loft and entertain myself there," Vic drawled in her slowest backwoods Tennessee accent. "But it isn't like the two of you are ever doing anything… sensitive… out in the open." She chuckled. "Y'all know you could have drop-in visitors any time."

The blond young woman sat down on one of the easy chairs, smiling at her boss.

"Long time no see," Erin said. Vic had driven her home in

Willie's truck after they had closed Auntie Clem's bakery for the day. Erin's car had been wrecked before Christmas and she hadn't yet replaced it. Vic didn't have a car of her own, but frequently borrowed Willie's. And it wasn't like they couldn't walk to and from Auntie Clem's if they needed to. It was only a few minutes away. Though neither of the menfolk liked them walking in the predawn hours when they had to start baking to have fresh bread and muffins in the case by the time they opened up to the early-morning customers. Bakers began the workday very early.

"Where's Willie?"

"He took the truck out to one of his claims." Vic shrugged. "I didn't get any details. Something important in the world of mines and minerals."

While Vic sometimes went spelunking with Willie on days off, she wasn't involved in his mining operations. Willie always had a dozen different jobs on the go and he sometimes kept strange hours, especially if Vic used his truck during the bakery hours.

"How is the mining life?" Erin asked. "Things… going well?"

"I have no idea. He doesn't tell me about it. He keeps his head above water, so I guess it's going well. Or his other ventures are going well. I don't get into any of the business details."

Erin nodded. She rolled her shoulders and rubbed her neck, trying to work out a few knots. Terry pushed her hands away and turned her so that her back was to him, so he could rub her muscles. Erin closed her eyes and rolled her neck, trying to relax into it. His fingers were hard, digging down into the muscles and trying to massage away the tightness.

"How's that?" he murmured close to her ear.

Erin nodded. "That's good." She was sore but, even though it hurt, she knew it would help later. "I'll do some tai chi before bed. And then I'll be nice and relaxed to sleep."

Terry's fingers paused for a moment, but he didn't disagree. Both of them had difficulty getting to sleep, but discussing how difficult it was and the likelihood that either of them would be able to get to sleep when they wanted to would not be productive.

And neither of them wanted to talk about it in front of Vic, either. She always noticed when Erin had a difficult night anyway.

"There was some mail for you," Erin told Vic, nodding to the side table. Even though they had a separate mailbox for the loft over the garage where Vic lived, the mailman didn't always get the mail sorted properly between the two boxes. Erin and Vic just passed mail back and forth as necessary and weren't really bothered by it.

Vic stretched out one of her long, slender arms and managed to snag the pile of envelopes. She sorted through it, pulling out the couple of mail pieces that were hers. One of them was just a bill, Erin had noticed, but the other looked like a personal letter. It was rare to get actual personal postal mail, so she couldn't help but notice. Everybody used email and social media.

Although that wasn't entirely true. Erin remembered that Vic had also gotten postal mail from an old girlfriend, crazy Theresa, someone that they all wanted to avoid running into again. Ever. There were warrants out for Theresa's arrest after the murder of Bo Biggles and her attack on Terry and Jack Ward when they had gone over to talk to her about it. But so far, she was in the wind and no one had been able to bring her to justice.

Erin eyed the envelope nervously. She didn't remember enough about Theresa's handwriting to know if it were the same writing or not. Theresa had known about Vic's gender transition but had thought that Vic would still be interested in renewing their relationship. Even though Vic was already in a committed relationship with Willie.

Vic examined the letter in the green envelope. She glanced over it at Erin. "What's wrong?"

"Nothing."

"You look like you're in pain. Terry, I think you're massaging too hard."

Terry stopped. He leaned forward, trying to see Erin's face. "Are you okay? You need to tell me if I'm hurting you."

"No." Erin gently rubbed the sore muscles that he had been

working on. "It wasn't that. I was just…" She shook her head. "Nothing. I just wondered who the letter was from. Not that it's any of my business. Just curious."

Vic's brows came down for a moment, and then she understood. "Oh! No, it's nothing to be worried about." She worked her finger into the corner of the envelope and slit it across. "It's not from… her."

"Oh." Erin swallowed and nodded. "That's good. I was just wondering. I know there's nothing to worry about, she's not going to show up here or start anything… she would risk getting caught and sent to prison for a few decades. She wouldn't do that."

"Crazy Theresa," Vic intoned, shaking her head. "You can never be sure what that one is going to do."

Erin's stomach clenched. Vic must have seen a change in her expression because she hurried to change her words.

"She wouldn't come here, though, you're right. She'll stay far away from Bald Eagle Falls and anyone who knows that there are warrants out for her. Maybe she'll go north to Canada."

Erin rolled her eyes and gave a little laugh. "To Canada? She'd freeze."

"Good. Maybe a little chill would be good for her."

Vic herself hadn't been too impressed with the northern weather when they had taken a cruise to Alaska. Born and bred in Tennessee, her blood was too thin to appreciate the cooler weather. She'd been chilled the whole time she'd been north of the forty-ninth parallel.

Vic pulled the paper out of the envelope and unfolded it. Her eyes scanned over the page. "Oh, it's Clayton." She raised her eyes to Erin and Terry. "He was one of the group on the cruise," she said. "One of the people I met onboard."

"Oh." Erin nodded and tried to look happy about this. She *was* happy that it wasn't from Theresa. But she couldn't help feeling a little twinge of disappointment that one of the LGBT group that Vic had made friends with on the cruise was sending Vic letters. Vic was already with Willie and she already had a best friend in Erin. She could have however many friends she liked, but Erin couldn't help feeling like the men and women that Vic had become friends with on the ship were somehow trying to wedge themselves between Vic and Erin.

That was ridiculous, of course. It didn't affect her friendship with Erin at all. But Erin had grown up without many friends and felt possessive. Vic shared experiences with the LGBT group that Erin would never have. Erin knew about the challenges that Vic went through living among the cis men and women in small-town, Bible-belt Tennessee, but she would never understand it with the same depth and nuance of people who had lived through it. Erin could never fully be a part of that side of Vic's life.

She would have to settle for being Vic's friend and working side-by-side with her.

"So, how is Clayton?" Erin asked, trying to inject warmth that she did not feel into the question.

Vic's eyes moved over the page. She didn't look up to answer Erin. "Good…"

Erin leaned back against Terry, resting into his warm body. She waited for more information from Vic. Vic's voice was far away, not really engaged with the conversation as she read Clayton's letter.

Terry resumed rubbing Erin's neck and shoulders, but with gentle hands this time, soothing the sore muscles. Maybe he understood how disconnected Erin felt from Vic at times like that. She felt like the little girl left at home when the others went out to play. Erin scratched at a drop of bread batter that had dried on her slacks. She wasn't sure how it had managed to get past her apron. She always seemed to have a few spatters that made it to her street clothes.

"He's coming to Bald Eagle Falls," Vic said.

"Coming here? Why would he be coming here?" Erin answered too quickly before she thought through her answer.

Vic looked over the letter at her again, eyebrows quirked,

shaking her head. "Why not? There's no reason he *couldn't* come here."

"No, I didn't mean that. I just meant I was surprised. It's sort of out of anyone's way. Is he coming just to see you, or is he on his way to something else…?"

"There's some kind of contest. He knows that you and I got the tickets to the cruise as part of a prize package, so he says maybe we can give him some pointers on how to win…"

"We?"

"You and me. We did win it together."

"Did he say me? Or just you?"

Vic's eyes went back to the letter. "Does it matter?"

"No. Of course not. Just curious. I don't think he really wants my input, does he?"

"I don't know. I doubt if he really wants anyone's advice. It's just something to say. Small talk."

Erin nodded. "Yeah, I guess. What contest is it? I hadn't heard anything about a contest. Is it in the city?"

"I don't know. I haven't heard of it before. Not one of the big ones like the Pillsbury Bake-Off or something. There are little ones running all the time."

"I guess."

"Especially in the rural areas around here. It's entertainment. A good way to get people together. Have some fun, raise some money. Make people remember your name for the next time that they're buying groceries at the store."

The Fall Fair was the first baking contest that Erin had ever entered, but she had noticed since then little contests that popped up here and there.

"I think we just got lucky with our entry. It wasn't like I really knew what I was doing."

"It wasn't just luck," Vic disagreed. "We worked hard on that cake. It was the perfect selection for the Fall Fair."

Erin's cheeks warmed a little. Vic had been instrumental in picking out their entry and teaching Erin about the traditional way to make it, but it had been Erin's recipe and execution. They had both contributed. But she was glad that Vic didn't think it was just luck that had gotten them the prize.

"When is he coming?"

Vic looked at her phone face. "Uh… in just a couple of weeks. I'll have to give him a call and make sure he has everything he needs while he is down for the contest and make sure that he is going to come by for a visit."

Cold as Ice Cream, Book #13 of the *Auntie Clem's Bakery* series by P.D. Workman can be purchased at pdworkman.com

ABOUT THE AUTHOR

Award-winning and USA Today bestselling author P.D. (Pamela) Workman writes riveting mystery/suspense and young adult books dealing with mental illness, addiction, abuse, and other real-life issues. For as long as she can remember, the blank page has held an incredible allure and from a very young age she was trying to write her own books.

Workman wrote her first complete novel at the age of twelve and continued to write as a hobby for many years. She started publishing in 2013. She has won several literary awards from Library Services for Youth in Custody for her young adult fiction. She currently has over 50 published titles and can be found at pdworkman.com.

Born and raised in Alberta, Workman has been married for over 25 years and has one son.

~

Please visit P.D. Workman at pdworkman.com to see what else she is working on, to join her mailing list, and to link to her social networks.

~

If you enjoyed this book, please take the time to recommend it to other purchasers with a review or star rating and share it with your friends!

facebook.com/pdworkmanauthor

twitter.com/pdworkmanauthor

instagram.com/pdworkmanauthor

amazon.com/author/pdworkman

bookbub.com/authors/p-d-workman

goodreads.com/pdworkman

linkedin.com/in/pdworkman

pinterest.com/pdworkmanauthor

youtube.com/pdworkman

www.ingramcontent.com/pod-product-compliance
Lightning Source LLC
Chambersburg PA
CBHW021320190726

48288CB00003B/891